For Love and Honor

D0869565

ALSO BY CATHY MAXWELL

The Seduction of Scandal
His Christmas Pleasure
The Marriage Ring
The Earl Claims His Wife
A Seduction at Christmas
In the Highlander's Bed
Bedding the Heiress
In the Bed of a Duke
The Price of Indiscretion
Temptation of a Proper Governess
The Seduction of an English Lady
Adventures of a Scottish Heiress
The Lady Is Tempted
The Wedding Wager
The Marriage Contract
A Scandalous Marriage
Married in Haste
Because of You
When Dreams Come True
Falling in Love Again
You and No Other
Treasured Vows
All Things Beautiful

THE CHATTAN CURSE
Lyon's Bride

Coming Soon
The Scottish Witch

ALSO BY LYNNE HINTON

Fiction
Pie Town

Friendship Cake
Hope Springs
Forever Friends
Christmas Cake
Wedding Cake

The Things I Know Best
The Last Odd Day
The Arms of God

Nonfiction
Meditations for Walking

Writing as Jackie Lynn
Down by the Riverside
Jacob's Ladder
Swing Low, Sweet Chariot

ALSO BY CANDIS TERRY

Second Chance at the Sugar Shack
Any Given Christmas

Coming Soon
Somebody Like You

For Love and Honor

CATHY MAXWELL

LYNNE HINTON

CANDIS TERRY

AVONIMPULSE

An Imprint of HarperCollins Publishers

Excerpt from *Lyon's Bride: The Chattan Curse* copyright © 2012 by Catherine Maxwell Inc.

Excerpt from *Welcome Back to Pie Town* copyright © 2012 by J. Lynne Hinton

Excerpt from *Second Chance at the Sugar Shack* copyright © 2011 by Candis Terry

EPub Edition JUNE 2012 ISBN: 9780062207692

Print edition ISBN: 9780062218162

10 9 8 7 6 5 4 3 2

Dear Reader,

We all honor the work that the heroic members of the military do and have done through the ages. With that in mind, I'm thrilled to present *For Love and Honor*, three novellas by three wonderful writers.

This collection came out of a brainstorming session. We wanted stories revolving around the theme of "military men." With that in mind, we approached three authors and told them to take the idea and run with it. What resulted are three unique romances, each special in its own way.

New York Times bestselling writer Cathy Maxwell tells a Regency-set tale. Lynne Hinton and Candis Terry's works are contemporary. But what they have in common is that they are deliciously romantic stories that I know you are all going to love.

Best,

Lucia Macro

Vice-President, Executive Editor

Avon Books

The Bookish Miss Nelson

CATHY MAXWELL

Chapter One

Spain, 1812

"AN OFFICER UNDER my command does not brawl like a common criminal, especially with the Irish." Colonel Medford hurled the words at Captain William Duroy as if they were rocks.

Heat flushed William's face. He had no regrets for jumping in the fray. The Irish had insulted his men, who had no choice but to defend their honor with their fists. They'd been outnumbered, and the Irish were not gentlemen. The fight had not been going in their favor until William had joined them, and then they had routed those sorry Irish bastards and taught them manners.

The Irish had been artillery men, and so the victory for the cavalry had been doubly sweet.

What William had not anticipated was for word to reach the prissy Medford. Even though Medford was his superior officer, he was of the same age and the two did not mesh well.

Medford was a younger son of a duke who had purchased his son's advancements. William's father was rich, having made his money in the service of the East India Company, but he was proud of his commoner roots. He believed his nine sons should work for their livings. For William, that meant earning field promotions.

"Suffice it to say there must be repercussions for your poor judgment," Medford said. He came around his desk to stand before William. He was a short man and had to look up to face William.

"You are hot-headed, Duroy. An officer under my command controls his temper. I want level heads around me. So, I'm going to have you cool your heels by undertaking a special mission." Medford placed his hands behind his back. "You will organize a small party of your men to escort our envoy to Spain's daughter back to Lisbon, where she will be sent home to England."

"*No*." The word burst from William before he had time to think clearly.

Medford's chin shot up in affront. William hurried to explain, "With all due respect, sir, we are preparing to meet the French any day now. I'm certain my presence, and that of my men, are needed here." Otherwise, he'd not have a chance at promotion. Thanks to Medford, he'd been a captain far too long.

The French and British armies had been shadowing each other for months. The event of it was in the air. Fortifications were being built and men moved with more purpose in the hot Spanish sun. After months of waiting and planning, the time was close at hand. He could not miss it.

"I want to fight," William said, the words hard to speak because he was begging.

"You have had your fight, Captain," Medford said, moving around his desk to his chair. "You chose to squander it on some Irish drunkards. I've already sent word to General Wellington that you will be escorting Sir Hew's daughter."

"Sir Hew Nelson?" William asked for clarification. "I'm to *escort* Miss Pippa Nelson?"

Medford smiled, the expression unpleasant. "I believe you unmarried lads refer to her as Bookworm Pippa, because she prefers having her nose in a book than admiring any of your antics."

William had never met her, but he'd heard plenty about her. She was her father's hostess and overly proud of her intellect. William didn't mind strong women. His mother was very independent. However, they said Pippa Nelson enjoyed showing men the sharp side of her tongue.

He'd also heard that her father had left her at Wellington's headquarters and departed on some mission without instructions on what was to be done with her. Apparently, the general had made his own decision.

"You are dismissed, Captain," Medford said, returning his attention to the papers on the desk in front of him.

And it was done. There was nothing else William could do. He was being banished days before what might be one of the most important battles against the French. He about-faced and walked out of the tent.

Medford's aide, Lieutenant Harris, was waiting for him outside with further instructions on the men he could take.

William listened in shock. The aide was an officer William considered a friend. He finished his instructions by advising, "The sooner you cart her to Lisbon, Duroy, the sooner you may return."

"I'll be too late for the battle," William said. "I can't believe this." The promotion was only a small part of why William wanted to return. He was a soldier. Soldiers fought. It was what they did.

"Well, if we vanquish the French in one battle and Napoleon surrenders completely, then yes," Harris said. "But I don't see that happening. It's possible you might make the battle if you return in time."

Could he make the trip to Lisbon and back in four to five days' time? Yes, if he pushed his men.

Determined now to make the best of the situation, William ordered Harris to send word to Miss Nelson to prepare to leave immediately.

He then picked a party of eight of his men to accompany him. He briefed them himself. "We don't want to miss our opportunity at Boney on Spanish soil, lads. We will make this trip to Lisbon and back inside a week. Choose the best horses and be prepared to ride in an hour."

Mounting his horse, Valiant, William rode over to Wellington's headquarters. The area around the building was a hive of activity, with aides hurrying this way and that. As William rode up, a huge, heavy overland coach pulled by two tired nags was driven in front of the building. Behind it came a groom holding a very pretty chestnut mare and a serviceable bay.

William took one look at the coach and had a sinking feeling. "What is this?" he asked one of the ostlers driving the coach.

"The possessions of Miss Nelson," the driver said. He glanced around and then confided, "It's nothing but books." He spit on the ground.

William had nothing against books. He was quite a reader himself. But he could not make good time to Lisbon with this overladen coach.

"Are you my escort?" a woman's imperial voice asked from the headquarters doorway. "You did not allow very much time for myself or Lilly to prepare."

Turning, William found himself face-to-face with Bookworm Pippa. She was not what he'd expected. He'd pictured her a lean, shriveled spinster.

Instead, he faced a petite, brown-eyed redhead with an abundance of freckles over her nose and cheeks. She wore a dashing green riding habit and a wide-brimmed hat set at a jaunty angle.

Lilly was obviously the name of her maid. She, too, was dressed to ride.

William bowed. "I am Captain William Duroy of the Seventh Light Dragoons. I am to be your escort, Miss Nelson."

She looked William up and down with the expression

one usually reserved for rat catchers. It was a novel experience for him. A woman had never reacted to him in that manner.

Instead of being insulted, he found himself amused.

"I do not go willingly," she announced with all the martyred drama of an actress on the stage.

"Neither do I, my lady," William said candidly.

Her lips parted in surprise. "Then don't take me," she said.

"We both have orders and very little choice. Shall we make the best of matters, Miss Nelson?"

Her expressive brows came together. "What if I chose not to go? What if I stayed right here and waited for my father? He expects me to be here."

William was aware that many were listening to this exchange. He had no doubt that Miss Nelson with her high-handed ways had created a good deal of uproar in a military headquarters. She was a lovely woman but seemingly unaware of her allure. There was too much combativeness in her stance, like a horse that had been mistreated and now expected the worst.

He found himself wondering what, or who, had hurt her to make her so distrustful.

Or what sort of man would go off and leave his daughter in a military encampment?

However, he was not in the mood to cure Miss Nelson of her problems. Keeping his voice pleasant, he said, "Then I would have to pick you up and carry you to that coach."

A hint of challenge came to her eyes. "You would not dare."

"I have orders, Miss Nelson. I most certainly would."

She took his measure, and then said, "I'm not riding in the coach. I shall ride."

"Excellent," William said. "I was going to order the books removed from the vehicle anyway."

"No. My books will come with me. They go everywhere I go."

"Except this time," William said, putting steel in his voice. "We must make good time to Lisbon."

"They go or I will *not* go," she replied, throwing down the gauntlet.

William felt his temper rise. "That is not an option." He turned to the driver. "Take the coach away. See that Miss Nelson's books are stored someplace safe—"

"There is no place safe," she interrupted him. "The French are coming."

"The French don't want your books. The command will see they are stored."

Her gloved hands formed fists. "I have collected these books over years. They are invaluable to me."

"Your life is invaluable to me," William answered. "Do as I say," he said to the driver. "Have a horse prepared with the ladies' possessions. Make it a good one. We have a hard ride ahead of us."

"Stay where you are," Miss Nelson said to the ostlers who had moved forward to obey William. They ignored her and followed his instructions.

William felt satisfaction, until he noticed the tears welling in Miss Nelson's eyes. He understood all too well just how frustrating it was to not have control over one's fate.

She reached and swiped the tears away, her stubborn chin rising. Only then did she see that he'd noticed. She scowled her opinion of him and went over to mount her horse with the help of a groom. He was not surprised to see she would be riding the chestnut.

William told himself he shouldn't be concerned about Miss Nelson. She was merely being head-strong. He would make Lisbon and back in time to fight. He would.

He just wished he hadn't seen her tears, because he had a feeling she was not the sort to give up easily.

And if Medford had planned to make William pay for his sins, he could not have found a better way than by saddling him with Miss Pippa Nelson.

Chapter Two

PIPPA NEVER THOUGHT she could so intensely dislike someone as much as she did the arrogant young officer tasked with marching her to Lisbon.

He was a bully, like so many of them. Men, especially young ones, were hard-hearted and selfish. They didn't understand her. No one did.

She had no trouble keeping up the bruising pace the officer had set. Her maid Lilly was not as fortunate. Lilly didn't like to ride, another crime Pippa placed at the officer's feet.

Oh, he was handsome with his dark hair and blue eyes that seemed to go right to the heart of a person. But Pippa's experience was that the more handsome the man, the more conceited he was. And this Captain Duroy was probably the worst of the lot. Her father had warned her about those sorts of men. He'd told her they could be beasts.

She was so busy engaging her mind in a litany of dislikes about him, she was surprised when he broke out of the riding formation to bring his horse in step with hers.

She kept her gaze on the road ahead.

"How are you faring, Miss Nelson?" he asked. "Are you still put out with me?"

She bit her tongue to keep from answering him. She'd learned early on that men thrived on attention. If she kept silent, he would leave her alone. That's what her father had advised her to do.

It was also easier to hide her own tongue-tiedness.

"I'm sorry about your books," he continued as if she had spoken. "However, the French are breathing down our necks, and we must move you to Lisbon with all due haste."

That was enough. Pippa had never been good at biting her tongue. It was her besetting sin. She had to speak her mind.

"We are traveling southward, Captain," she informed him coolly. She knew what was going on. She'd grown up in diplomatic and military circles and she listened well. "The French are nowhere close to here."

To her pleasure, his smile tightened.

"I have been around this war for a long time, sir," she said. "Do not patronize me. We were perfectly safe to bring my books with me. What I sense is that you wish to be done with the care of me and hurry back to your command so that you don't miss the fight. Am I wrong?"

"That is my purpose," he conceded.

"Yes, well, your purpose was against mine."

"And perhaps I understand you more than you believe."

That provocative statement caught her attention. "I doubt that. If you did, you would not be taking me to a ship that will deliver me to England."

"It's your homeland, Miss Nelson. You will be safe there. We want to see you protected."

"*Save* me from being *protected*," she declared. "You are a man. You don't know what it is like for a woman. My aunts and cousins have all these rules and are always lecturing me. I was born in Calcutta, raised in the Orient. When I return to England, I can't go anywhere without permission and I must always watch my tongue. I say the wrong things. Even here, amongst the soldiers, I know they believe I'm odd."

"They find you original," he corrected. "And you shouldn't let that bother you. My own mother is eccentric, independent and fiercely proud of it. There are women such as yourself in England. You just haven't met them yet."

"I doubt if I'll *ever* meet one. England can never provide the freedom my father gives me," she announced with a touch of defiance.

He appeared as if ready to challenge her statement, but then decided against it. Instead, he said, "I like your mare. She's an Arabian breed."

Pippa willingly changed the subject with him. "Tatiana is from Russia. A gift from one of my father's friends."

"Tatiana? What sort of a name is that for a horse?"

She was caught off guard by his criticism, but then

thought she saw laughter in his eyes. He was teasing her
. . . she thought. People rarely teased her.

"It's the name of the fairy princess in *A Midsummer
Night's Dream*," she said, and immediately regretted her
words, realizing she sounded haughty. He was English.
He would know the name. However, she had come off
sounding superior and stiff.

Usually, at this moment, people would start to with-
draw from her. Young men would frown, pout even.
Young women would giggle at her. She never knew how
to hit the right tone.

"I know who she is," he said, without taking offense,
"but a mare like that should have an English name."

"Like what?" Pippa asked, still uncertain.

"Buttercup."

"Like the flower?" Pippa frowned.

"And very English," he answered.

"Oh, and what English name do you have for your
horse?" she questioned, something that was always tight
and distrustful inside of her unwinding a bit.

"Valiant. Very English."

"Very heavy," she answered.

"So is Tatiana."

"But poetic," she demurred.

"Valiant is poetic."

"And a mouthful."

"Says the woman who named her horse Tatiana."

Pippa laughed, realizing the conversation had come
full-circle back to her. Captain Duroy was very clever
and entertaining—and she must beware. Her father had

warned her of just his sort. Keep them at a distance.

He noticed her change of mood. "What is it?"

She looked at him, at his easy good looks and the effortless way he rode. He was a horseman through and through. A dashing man. A dangerous one. A man much like the one who had run off with her mother.

"I don't like you," she said, speaking the words aloud to give them force.

He was taken aback. "Have I offended you?"

Pippa felt a bit ill to her stomach. Why had her father left her? Why was she dealing with this alone?

"Miss Nelson, is something the matter?"

She heard the concern in his voice and didn't want to trust him. She grabbed hold of the first halfway reasonable excuse to push him away. "You are making me do what I do not wish to do. And you took my books." She could hear herself, knew she sounded inane—and yet she must not let him close.

He didn't speak right away, and that made her cross. "Have you nothing to say?" She dared him to fight back. Then she could blame him for something.

"I say that Medford knew what he was doing when he chose you to be my punishment." With those cryptic words, he rose up the line to take his place . . . leaving her alone.

WILLIAM HAD A desire to needle Pippa Nelson, and he didn't understand why.

Perhaps it was because she gave off the air that she didn't need a man.

Perhaps it was because she was an attractive woman who didn't seem to notice him.

Or perhaps it was because she reminded him of his mother, a woman he greatly admired. She truly had an independent spirit.

So he kept his distance.

And it didn't seem to bother her.

One of his men, Sergeant Larson, found a small inn for them for the night. As William was organizing the sleeping arrangements, Lilly, Miss Nelson's maid, came to him with a question of when they would be expected to rise in the morning.

"Miss Pippa wishes to know," Lilly said. She was a middle-aged woman with apple cheeks and a friendly spirit.

"Tell her an hour before dawn," William answered.

"Very good, Captain." She started to leave but then stopped. "I saw you talking to her earlier today. You made her laugh."

"Is that so unusual?" William said.

Lilly took a step toward him, lowering her voice. "Her mother ran away with a Russian officer when Miss Pippa was ten. It's a tender age for a girl. They all need their mothers. I wasn't in Sir Hew's employ then. He thought to keep Pippa for himself. He cares for his daughter, but he can be a selfish man, and he shut out many after his wife left. I think if he had his way, he'd insist that Miss Pippa be at his beck and call for the rest of his life."

"Why are you telling me this?"

"You made her laugh," Lilly repeated. "I was hired by

Miss Pippa's aunt, Lady Romley, because she fears for her niece's happiness. I'd begun to believe I'd arrived too late to save Miss Pippa, until I heard her laugh today. Please, don't be offended when she wards you off. In his anger at his wife's unfaithfulness, Sir Hew has put many strange notions in his daughter's head. She feels she must always prove her faithfulness to him."

"A father should want his daughter to go forward with her life," William said.

"And I believe Miss Pippa's is a loving nature. Sir Hew is not a loving man. But I've said too much. If I have trespassed on your good nature, forgive me."

"No, Lilly, I appreciate this information."

"I thought you would, Captain."

William set sentries. He would check on them through the night. He turned in. He was usually a good sleeper, but he found that this night, thoughts of a brown-eyed, opinionated redhead kept him awake. So he was a bit groggy the next morning, and yet anxious to see Pippa Nelson.

However, when he strode into the inn's dining room, Miss Nelson was not there. Instead, a tearful Lilly came running down the hall for him.

"What has she done now?" William asked. "Don't tell me she refuses to come with us. I will go up and fetch her."

"It's worse than that, Captain," Lilly said. "She's not in her bed, and her horse is gone. The innkeeper tells me his son is missing his clothes. Miss Pippa has stolen them, and she's left."

Chapter Three

YES, IT WAS dangerous for a woman to be riding alone, but Pippa was determined to return to the British encampment. That was where her father had left her, and that was where he'd expect her to be. Besides, she would not return to London. She wouldn't. It had become a matter of pride now. Or so she'd thought.

A small part of her realized that she could possibly be running from Captain Duroy and his disturbing presence. He knew how to slip past her guard. He threatened her sense of well-being in a way she didn't quite understand.

So, it was time for daring action.

And daring women did not sit back and wait for others to make decisions.

She had stolen the innkeeper's son's clothes to disguise herself as a boy. Since she was small-busted, she hoped wearing the lad's loose-fitting shirt would be enough to let her pass as a male. She'd hidden the vibrant color of her hair by wrapping a white scarf around her head. She'd also taken her wide-brimmed hat to hide her freckles from the sun and passersby, but it had flown off her head in the night, and she'd not wanted to waste the time to search for it.

Pippa had a small stash of coins in a leather bag which she wore around her neck. She'd tucked a small dirk inside her riding boots. By her estimation, riding Tatiana at a good clip, she could return to the camp by late midday.

Mayhap her father was already there and wondering what had happened to her?

If he wasn't, she'd just have to work her way around General Wellington. Perhaps in taking the desperate step of running away, the general would understand that she truly did not want to be packed off to England.

She hoped Captain Duroy would not pay a price for her decision, and it bothered her to think that he might.

The captain would come after her. Of course he would. That was why she had to be certain she outrode him.

What she hadn't realized was how tired both she and Tatiana were. Her loyal mare tried to keep up the pace, but after traveling the day before neither of them had the energy to push hard.

Soon, they were walking.

The Spanish sun beat down on Pippa's head. She could feel herself freckling. Right there was reason enough to not go to London. Her cousins called her freckles "spots," a derogatory term if ever she'd heard one. Pippa liked the sun and hated all the fussing her aunts had made in trying to use creams to make her freckles fade.

She didn't look at anyone she passed on the road. Nor did she dare stop. She pushed herself, and she pushed Tatiana—until she could push no more. By late morning, the heat and sun were too much for both her and her poor horse. She came to a small village. There was a well in the center of the town. She gave Tatiana water, ignoring the curious looks of the few people who were out on the street.

Pippa knew she was going to have to find food for herself and give Tatiana a rest, and she thought she had time. She'd chosen a different route from the one Captain Duroy had them travel the day before. She hoped that when he came after her, he'd think her silly enough to return by that route and so would miss stopping her before she reached the British camp.

A few inquiries directed her to a small inn on the edge of the village. Old men sat in the shade of a tree in the front yard. They watched her ride up and began speaking in low voices to each other. Pippa listened hard to hear if they recognized she was a woman. They didn't. She was safe. They only admired her precious horse.

She tied Tatiana to a post and entered the inn, keeping her head down.

If the innkeeper inside, a rotund man with a weathered face, noticed her sex, he didn't say. Instead, he took her money for hay for Tatiana and sent a lad out to feed the horse. He then went off to prepare Pippa's request for soup and bread.

The inn appeared clean enough. She wasn't the only one in the main room. There was a table of young men, workers actually, enjoying their wine. They didn't seem to pay her any attention.

Just to be safe, she took a seat on the other side of the room from them and kept her scarf on her head. She yawned but didn't feel a need to sleep. This was her grandest adventure. She was on her own. Completely.

Yes, there was danger, but she was not afraid. As she waited for her food, she thought of all the things her father had warned her against. This would certainly be one of them, but then here she was and she felt quite bold.

The innkeeper thought to bring her some cold chicken and cheese as well as the soup. Pippa fell upon the food. She didn't think she'd ever been so hungry before. Outside the window, she could see Tatiana munching on her hay with the same energy Pippa had for her meal, and life felt good—until she saw Captain Duroy striding from the village.

He was just walking down the road, the sun shining off the silver buttons of his uniform. He was heading straight for the inn.

Panic erased her appetite.

The captain would know she was here. He'd recognize Tatiana immediately.

Pippa jumped up from her chair and ran out into the hall, almost knocking over the innkeeper. She raced down the hall and around a corner. There was a door. She opened it and discovered a small storage room. It was really little more than a pantry with slatted doors.

Here was where the oils and wine, the onions, peppers, and olives were kept. Pippa squeezed herself inside and waited.

She didn't have a plan other than the hope that Captain Duroy would believe she'd run off and perhaps she could go to Tatiana and escape.

And then she heard booted footsteps on the inn's wooden floor. She held her breath.

Captain Duroy asked the innkeeper in very poor Spanish where the Englishwoman was.

The innkeeper sounded genuinely confused, not only by Captain Duroy's Spanish but by his insistence that there was a woman in the inn. Then the captain asked if a young boy had entered the inn. Pippa wrapped her arms around her waist, waiting, praying, and fearing the innkeeper would give an honest answer.

Booted steps started walking in her direction. She closed her eyes, listening and hoping that the captain would walk right down the hall and not see her little hiding spot.

There was a moment when she could not hear his steps.

She opened her eyes—and then she saw his shadow outside the cupboard door.

He opened the door. "Hello, Miss Nelson."

Pippa grabbed ahold of the shelving around her and braced her legs. "I'm not returning with you. I won't go."

"Oh, you will come with me," he said, his voice frighteningly calm. "You don't have a choice. Hmmmm, this is odd," he said as if struck by some thought of fancy. "I believe we had this same conversation yesterday, did we not?"

"Yes, when you threatened violence against me."

He laughed. "And obviously you didn't believe I was a man of my word."

Pippa gripped the shelves harder. "I shall create a terrible scene."

"I'm certain of it." He took a step into the storage room, reaching for her waist.

Pippa opened her mouth, ready to scream for help—when the sound of male French voices interrupted them.

Instantly the two of them were quiet.

The newcomers were shouting for the innkeeper in Spanish.

Captain Duroy moved into the storage room with her, closing the door behind them. The space was very tight. They were thigh-to-thigh, chest-to-chest.

"Who do you think it is?" she whispered.

He placed an arm across her as if to protect her. "Soldiers." He listened a moment.

She strained to hear all she could, as well.

There were more booted steps. This wasn't a small party of men. It sounded as if the inn was being invaded.

Pippa rose on her toes so she could speak in his ear. "I didn't believe the French were this far south of our troops."

"They aren't supposed to be," he answered. "How is your French?"

"As excellent as my Spanish. How is yours?"

"As terrible as my Greek, which is better than my

Spanish," he said. Only he would tease in this moment.

The men in the main room were officers. They complained of the march south, of the laziness of their men, and of how hungry they were. The order to the innkeeper was to keep the wine coming. They were thirsty men who had been long on the road.

Someone mentioned admiring the horse outside, and he was ordered to take it.

They couldn't have Tatiana. Pippa surged toward the door. Captain Duroy's arms stopped her. He shook his head, warning her to be wise.

She leaned in against his chest, needing someone else's strength right now. "What of your horse?"

"I don't know." He didn't remove the arm he'd placed around her. "I left him in the village with some boys. I can only hope they've hidden him."

Suddenly, Pippa's grand adventure became frighteningly real.

The wool of his uniform jacket was rough against her cheek as she buried her face against it. Tatiana was all she had of what she valued. They'd already taken away her books.

She wanted to push Captain Duroy away, and yet she discovered she desperately needed him for support. He *did* understand.

The French were relaxing. Several of the men complained of their mission. They sounded confident that the English were not a threat and didn't understand why they had to come this far south to meet troops that would not be needed.

Pippa whispered, "Do you understand some of what they are saying?"

Captain Duroy nodded grimly.

At that moment, the door to the storage room opened.

The captain clamped a hand over Pippa's mouth as she started to gasp in surprise.

It was good that he had. The innkeeper had been the one to open the door. He raised a finger to his lips. Captain Duroy nodded.

The innkeeper reached in past them for some onions and a curing ham. He shut the door.

Pippa almost collapsed with relief, but it was short-lived. Suddenly, she began shaking. A hundred fears assailed her at once. They would be discovered. They could not stay here forever hiding. Her father would be furious if she was captured. She could not let them know who she was, but if she didn't what would become of her? Her father had told her horrible stories of what the soldiers did to women—

"Don't give in to your fear," Captain Duroy ordered.

"How can I not?" she answered.

"Think of something else."

"Like what?" Her mind was filled with nothing but the stories she'd been told. They would kill Captain Duroy. They would behead him right before her. They would behead her.

"What do you most enjoy?" he said. "Think on it. What is your favorite time of year, and what would you be doing?"

She shook her head.

"What is your favorite novel?" he persisted. "What book would you choose out of all of them?"

Pippa attempted to focus on her books. *Pamela*, *Robinson Crusoe*, *The Lady of the Lake*, *Castle Rackrent*. . .

"Have you been to any plays? What of Shakespeare?" he continued, and then he made an exasperated sound, because speaking of Shakespeare reminded her of her beloved horse and he was aware of it.

Who knew what the French would do to her? The tears she'd been holding back escaped and ran down her cheeks.

She felt such a fool—

Her thoughts were cut short when Captain Duroy turned her face up to his, and brought his lips down over hers.

Chapter Four

PIPPA HAD NEVER been kissed before, and she'd never imagined it would be like this. People in books didn't kiss surrounded by onions and olives.

And books left out many details.

The only way she could describe Captain Duroy's kiss is that it was something akin to a fish grabbing a worm. Her mouth was the worm . . . and she didn't know if she liked it.

She pressed her lips together.

He slid his tongue along them as if asking her to open to him.

The contact shocked her. She pulled away.

He had his hand at the small of her back so she couldn't move very far without hitting her head on some sausage hanging from the shelf. He pulled her back to him. Her breasts flattened against his chest, and she found it hard to breathe. He was so tall, so commanding. So handsome.

His lips next to her ear, he said, "You are not supposed to kiss someone with your lips all pressed together as if you are tasting something disagreeable."

"I wouldn't know," she said, heat rising into her cheeks.

"Well, I'm trying to educate you."

She looked up at him. "Why would you want to do that?"

He smiled. "To take your mind off your fear. Keep your courage, Miss Nelson. You've been brave so far. Don't give up yet."

"But what if they find us?"

"They won't."

He sounded so certain that she let herself believe.

And he had called her brave.

No one had ever done that. Usually, she'd been referred to as a nuisance.

But he didn't kiss her again, and her active mind started wondering what it was she should learn. And how could she ask him to teach her?

Instead, Captain Duroy was more interested in the French. "I understand some of what they are saying, but not enough to keep up with them. Do you understand everything?"

She nodded.

"Tell me."

Pippa started interpreting, ferreting information from amongst the talk of women, teasing of others' foibles, and general complaints. They were apparently delivering supplies of ammunition to troops coming up from

Italy. They were to meet the troops on the morrow in a village called Bejar. Pippa didn't understand what it all meant, but the captain did.

To her relief, the soldiers finally left.

That's when she realized exactly how close she was standing to Captain Duroy and that she had grabbed his sleeve and had been holding tight.

She released her hold. "I'm sorry," she murmured and started to open the door.

He caught her hand and turned her around to face him. "Don't run," he said.

"Run?"

The captain shook his head as if annoyed with her. "It is all right to be human," he said. "And it is acceptable to be afraid when the situation warrants it."

"You weren't afraid."

"Why do you think I kissed you?" he said. "I had to take my mind off my fear with something I wanted to do."

He didn't wait for her reaction to that startling pronouncement but opened the door and let them both out. He kept hold of her hand.

"Still," she said as she followed him, "there are ways a gentlewoman must behave." She was far too aware of him. He smelled of the fresh air and a spicy scent uniquely his own.

"Especially the gentlewomen dressed in breeches," he remarked, looking around the hallway corner to be certain it was safe to leave their haven.

She felt herself blush. "Even in breeches," she remarked, gently pulling her hand from his.

Captain Duroy cocked an eyebrow. "Rubbish," he answered.

Pippa opened her mouth to be offended, but then realized she didn't know what to say. She did believe most of the rules of society were rubbish. Certainly they didn't have a place here.

"You aren't like the other men of my acquaintance," she admitted before she could stop herself.

"Men can be free thinkers, too," he tossed over his shoulder as he walked down the hallway.

"No, I believe you may be unique," she murmured, and he shot her a grin.

"There is hope for you yet, Miss Nelson." He opened the front door just as the innkeeper poked his head around the corner and then walked into the tap room. The man started cursing.

"What is he saying?" Captain Duroy asked.

"The soldiers didn't pay him. He's calling them names."

"Tell him I agree with him," the captain ordered as he reached for his money purse. "I'll pay their bill."

"You will?"

He frowned. "If I have enough."

"I have some." She began to remove her money bag from the cord around her neck.

"Save your money," he ordered. "You may need it."

"And you won't? Why? What are you planning to do?"

"I'm going to destroy the ammunition on that supply train." He gave the money to the innkeeper, who immediately began praising him for his generosity.

But Pippa was stunned. "You plan on doing this yourself?"

The captain nodded, the set of his mouth telling her he wasn't jesting. "What is the innkeeper saying now?"

Pippa shook her head, trying to bring herself back to her Spanish. "He appreciates what you've done."

"Good," Captain Duroy said. "Tell him I expect him to take care of you as if you were his own daughter until I return."

"What?" Pippa looked incredulously at him. "Do you plan to leave me here?"

"Until I return. Or until the English come through here. I want you safe."

But Pippa had other plans. "You are not leaving me here. I will go with you."

He shook his head. "Absolutely not." He started to walk toward the door.

Pippa rushed to put herself in his path. "You will not leave without me."

"I must. What I'm going to do is dangerous."

"So you will go out there and do it alone? You mustn't. You can't. It's madness."

"It's my duty."

He would have gone around her, but Pippa was made of stern stuff. She pressed her hand against his chest. "They stole my horse. I am going after *her*."

"I shall try and bring her to you." He again attempted to go forward. Pippa wouldn't let him.

"We go *together*," she said. "It is what the British do.

I cannot stay here cooling my heels when I could be of some service to you."

"Miss Nelson—" he started in a placating voice.

She cut him off. "Don't patronize me, Captain. As a family member of a British envoy, I am considered part of the military."

"I doubt that—"

"I don't." She softened her tone. "Let me help you, *please*. I know very little about what you have in mind, but you will need an extra pair of hands, to hold your horse if nothing else. Or to tell the world what you set out to do if you fail."

She'd caught his attention then. "I won't fail," he assured her.

"We go together," she answered.

He drew a breath and then released it, muttering something about willful females before saying, "Come along then."

Pippa happily complied.

The lads who had watched his horse had served him well. They told Pippa that the French had been taking whatever they wished from the villagers, but the boys had hidden Valiant in the church and he'd not been discovered.

Since Captain Duroy had given all his money to the innkeeper, Pippa proudly paid the lads for their resourcefulness. This time he didn't tell her to keep her money.

Within moments, they were on their way in the direction of Bejar.

It wasn't hard to follow the supply train. The French

were confident. They had controlled Spain for too long to believe they needed to look over their shoulder.

"Do we have a plan?" Pippa asked as they rode. She sat behind them on the horse, her arms around his waist.

"None yet," he said, "other than to destroy all their ammunition. Without it, the French can't attack us from the rear."

"How will you move close to it?"

"I will have to think of a diversion," he said.

Tired, Pippa laid her head against his back. He didn't seem to mind, and it felt good to be here with him.

Suddenly, Pippa understood what it meant to belong somewhere. She'd known Captain Duroy for less than forty-eight hours, and yet she found peace by his side.

"Do you know," she said, her voice low as she reasoned this all out in her mind, "that kiss we had, it was nothing like what I've read about in books. The authors don't explain the details."

There was a beat of silence, and then he said, "Then remind me that I need to show you the details. I wouldn't want you to miss the experience."

Her heart skipped a funny beat. "I think that sort of kiss might be more interesting than any I've read about in books," she admitted.

"Trust me, Miss Nelson, before this night is through, you shall discover there are many things in life more exhilarating than anything you can read in a book."

Her cheek against his back, she could readily concede she had already discovered what he said was true.

WILLIAM KNEW IT was madness to bring Miss Nelson with him, except she had been right—he did need another person to help.

But also, he liked her. It felt good to have her with him. She didn't complain and was game for anything. He also didn't mind her body this close to his.

Perhaps he shouldn't have kissed her. It had not been a good kiss at all, and yet he couldn't stop thinking about it. Her honest innocence was refreshing.

Yes, he was still angry she had run away. That had been dangerous, foolish . . . and also showed her courage. He was not accustomed to thinking of women as having courage, but Miss Nelson was proving him wrong on several points.

And if he kept thinking about her, he'd see them both killed.

Destroying the ammunition in the French supply train was necessary. In truth, he might not survive this encounter, but he was a soldier first and foremost.

The French finally set up camp on a small plain. When William noticed that the dust and sounds of wagons and horses were growing closer, he reined in Valiant and moved well away from where the enemy would set up sentries. Tying his horse up, he and Miss Nelson enjoyed a quick meal of bread and cheese from the innkeeper.

He then set out to spy upon the French. Miss Nelson wanted to join him, but he made her stay behind.

Coming to a bluff, he crawled on his belly until he could look upon the French camp without being seen.

A second later, he heard a noise—a moment before Miss Nelson crawled on her belly beside him. "What shall we do?" she whispered.

"Don't you do anything I order you to do?" he demanded.

A dimple flashed at him in her smile. "What fun would that be?"

And in that moment, William tumbled in love.

It was a very odd thing. He'd never felt it before. His mother had always told him that when he met the girl he was meant to meet, he would know. Her prophecy had sounded like nonsense to him. He'd desired many women, but had not had that moment when he said, this is *the one*—until now.

"I want you to be safe," he said.

She nodded, her gaze shifting from him to the French encampment, which she studied like a seasoned mercenary. "I will be."

"I don't know that. You haven't listened to one order I've given."

Again she looked at him, and he thought she was adorable. The Spanish sun brought out her freckles, which seemed exactly right on her face. Perfect even.

He must be mad, because here they were in grave danger and he wanted to kiss her.

William blocked the idea from his mind. He should be wanting to *strangle* her.

He'd see them both killed if he didn't stop mooning over her.

Beyond her head, he saw movement.

The top of a helmet showed itself from the other side of the bluff, and William knew they were seconds away from being discovered by the approaching soldier.

Chapter Five

PIPPA NOTICED IMMEDIATELY when Captain Duroy's attention veered from her. She turned and saw the Frenchman coming over the bluff.

In seconds, the sentry would see them. All would be lost.

And then Pippa knew what she would do. Captain Duroy wanted a diversion. Well, she would create one.

Before he could stop her, she rose to her feet and began walking toward the sentry. She pulled the scarf from her hair. Her copper curls sprung free in joyous abandon.

Of course the guard saw her and immediately crouched, his bayonet ready to run her through. Pippa stopped and thrust out her chest. Now was the time to show that *she* did have breasts.

"I am the daughter of Sir Hew Nelson, the British envoy to Spain. I insist on being taken to your commander."

The Frenchman frowned. She'd deliberately spoken in English. Let them find out later she was fluent in their language. She also expected the sight of a woman in male attire would protect Captain Duroy. She was right. The guard had no eyes for anyone but her.

"*Allez*," he ordered, waving her in front of him with his bayonet.

She held up her hands to show she had no tricks and walked forward. However, she could not resist a glance in Captain Duroy's direction.

He was not there.

She had been a very good diversion.

It turned out that the guard had wandered away from his post to heed a call to nature. That is what he told his comrades as he proudly marched his captive into the camp.

The ammunition wagons, heavily loaded with kegs of gunpowder and the other needs of war, were in a circle in the middle of the camp, the tents arranged around them.

She made certain to hold her head high as she was paraded around. She wanted all eyes on her. She was like brave Boudicca, confronting her Roman enemies, or one of the goddesses of Olympus, unafraid. She also knew that, if she had any inkling of Captain Duroy's character, he was thinking of a way to reach those wagons—and she trusted he would come for her as well.

However, her facade fell away as they approached the commander of the supply train. He was a short man with blondish hair and narrow, almost evil eyes. He was also evaluating her horse so intently, running his hand up and down Tatiana's leg, he didn't notice Pippa and the guardsman at first.

Tatiana nickered at Pippa's arrival. Pippa wanted to run to her beloved horse and throw her arms around the mare's neck, but she stood her ground.

The commander looked up, and then his gaze brightened. "What have we here?" he asked in French.

The guard told his story. By now a large crowd had gathered around them. Pippa tried to pretend she did not understand the crude comments made about her. Several men talked about her legs. Pippa found that interesting. She hadn't realized legs on a woman were so desirable. A few complained of her lack of endowment, but instead of being insulted she thought of Captain Duroy. He didn't mind her lack of an overabundant chest.

And she wondered what he was doing now. She hoped he was still safe—

The explosion behind her let her know that not only was he safe, he was close at hand.

Men cried out as debris hit them. Several turned to save the other wagons, but those, too, exploded.

Tatiana was frightened. She reared, pulling the lead rope out of her handler's hand.

Pippa did not waste a moment but moved closer to her horse, even as she saw Captain Duroy. He was running from the explosions and fires that were quickly spreading to the tents.

Soldiers saw him and cried out to stop him. No one was paying attention to Pippa any longer.

"Tatiana, heed me," she ordered.

The mare pranced but stilled enough for Pippa to throw herself on her back. She grabbed her mane, put her heels to her horse, and went charging to rescue the captain.

He was in a fight with several soldiers. He'd managed to find a sword and now defended himself from two soldiers while the rest were running around madly trying to put out the fires.

But they were too late. The last wagon exploded.

"Captain, here!" Pippa yelled out over the roar of flames.

He'd seen her coming. "Keep going," he said.

"Not without you."

He surprised her then by pulling a small pistol from his uniform pocket and firing it at the soldier nearest him. The man dropped, and Captain Duroy had enough time to launch himself up behind Pippa. Together, they rode as hard as they could to where Valiant was tethered.

"Can you continue to ride bareback?" the captain asked.

"Of course," Pippa said.

He smiled, his expression saying he'd never doubted she could, and she was filled with fierce pride.

They rode then, hard and fast. Their horses wanted as much distance from the fire as they did. They raced over hills and across plains until at last they came to a village.

The hour was very late, but there were still some people out. There was no inn, but a widow rented a room and had stabling for their horses.

The whole time, Pippa felt as if her emotions were

on edge. She didn't even think twice when the widow assumed the two of them were man and wife. In fact, she couldn't draw a decent breath until they were in the safety of the bedroom.

Captain Duroy whirled her around to face him. "That was the most foolhardy stunt you have pulled yet. You should never have put yourself in such danger."

Taken aback, Pippa felt her temper ignite. He should be thanking her. "It worked, didn't it?"

He took her by both arms, as if he would shake her. "But it easily could have been a disaster. Miss Nelson, Pippa, if you ever do anything like that again, I shall—"

"You shall what?" she dared him.

The anger in his expression suddenly eased, and in its place was an emotion she couldn't quite define, until he said, "I shall kiss you."

Before the meaning of his words formed in her brain, he was kissing her—and this time she didn't hold her lips closed.

She was wiser now. She opened her mouth and kissed him right back.

And what a kiss it was! Who could have imagined a simple kiss could carry such meaning, such power? It was as if they breathed in each other's souls . . . and she was lost.

"Pippa," he whispered. She adored hearing him say her name.

He started to pull away. She threw her arms around his neck, holding him close, and answered, "Yes, William. Yes."

Some things were not the same in life as what she'd read in books. She now knew *They kissed* was tame in comparison with actually kissing, and she wondered what else she didn't know.

Her father had warned that men could be beasts. She now decided that could be a very good thing.

Their kiss deepened. He was holding her, his hands at her waist.

She found she wanted more. She wanted to be completely in his arms without any barriers between them. She began unbuttoning his uniform.

His lips brushed her forehead. "Don't, Pippa."

"Yes, William." She found the buttons of his breeches, and his protests stopped.

They made love.

And Pippa thought this was the most beautiful thing she'd experienced in her life.

Here was a man she could admire. A gallant man. One filled with courage.

He took great care of her.

The thought passed through her mind that if they had not just come so close to death, he might have considered twice about claiming her. She was glad he didn't.

Having him deep inside her body fulfilled her in a way she'd not believed possible. Years of self-doubt, fear, and insecurity were vanquished in her lover's arms.

He spoke to her. He said her name as if it was a blessing.

Her body responded to him with a will all its own. But there was something else at work here. Pippa felt as if she was meant to meet this man, to be here in his arms.

He was her fate, her destiny—and as their bodies worked together, as he initiated her into the rites of love, taking from her that which was only hers to give, she discovered the pure bliss of pleasure. And she learned pleasure's depth as well. Two shall become one. She now understood what those words meant.

For a long, long time, she could not speak. He didn't move, either, except to ease his body off of hers and then gather her close. She laid her head on his chest, feeling his heartbeat return to normal.

He spoke, his fingers playing with her curls. "I want you to return to England." Before she could protest, he continued, "I must know you are safe, Pippa. I will send you to my mother. She's very forward-thinking, and my father worships her. I adore her."

Pippa rested her hand on his chest. "Do you think you could adore me?"

He pretended to consider the matter a moment and then confessed, "I already do."

No words could be sweeter to her. She swallowed and then took a risk. "I think I love you," she answered.

"I know I love you."

His words hadn't been a mistake. He cared for her. Truly cared for her. This strong, noble, honorable man loved her. She finally found words to speak. "Is making love always like it was with us, William?"

"It's never been like that before," he answered. "Only with you."

Only with her. Magic words. "Can we try it again, just to be certain?"

His response was to laugh, and then they did try again. Their lovemaking wasn't as good as it had been the first time.

It was *better*.

Chapter Six

THEY MARRIED VERY early the next morning.

William roused a priest who objected that the banns had not been read. William's response was to cut two of the silver buttons from his uniform to offer as payment, and the priest kept his silence. The padre did not even question the bride marrying while wearing breeches.

Pippa knew that they would have to remarry in the Church of England, but that morning, in the shadowy knave of a Catholic church, she spoke her vows and meant them with all her heart.

Together they rode to join William's men. Her maid, Lilly, was furious over her running away and had a few words for William when she learned they'd married. But they were happy ones.

"She will make you dance to a merry tune," she predicted.

"I pray that she does," William answered.

The rest of the trip to Lisbon was uneventful and yet

perfect. William had sent Sergeant Larson back to his superior officers with a report on the French supply train.

Pippa and William rode beside each other for the trip, talking about everything and talking about nothing. They didn't dawdle. William was anxious to return to his company before the fighting, but they didn't waste this precious time together, either.

All was good . . . until they reached Lisbon's port—where Pippa found her father waiting anxiously for her in the British port office.

He rushed up to her. "Pippa, my God, I have been worried to the point of illness over you."

"Didn't General Wellington or someone on his staff tell you where they'd sent me?" she asked, a bit overwhelmed. She hadn't yet thought of how she would break the news of William to her father. She wasn't certain how he would react. He could be so possessive.

"They said they sent you here with an escort." Her father looked past her shoulder. "Thank you, Captain, for seeing her safe. You are done here. Carry on."

Pippa drew a deep breath. "Father, there is something I must tell you. This is Captain William Duroy—"

"Duroy?" her father repeated, interrupting her. "The nabob? Up in Yorkshire?"

"My sire, sir," William answered. She was grateful that he was letting her handle this, although she sensed his impatience in her breaking the news. It was as if he understood her concerns.

In such a short time, they knew each other that well.

"Father, William is my husband." She took William's

arm. "And he is the best, most wonderful, bravest man I know, except for you, Papa."

Her father took a step back as if she'd struck him. The color left his face. "*No.*" He shook his head. "You cannot have married. Not without my permission."

William spoke. "I would have asked it, sir, if there had been time . . ." And that was when the story of her running away and blowing up French ammunition wagons was shared.

Her father did not take it well, and even though Pippa didn't speak of the lovemaking, he seemed to understand that more had happened than just a bit of fighting the French.

When he did find words, his voice was dark, guttural. "I shall have this marriage annulled. Immediately. And I shall see you stripped of all command and rank, Duroy. Come, Pippa, to the ship."

In the past, Pippa would have hurried to obey.

She didn't this time. She couldn't. She realized she was no longer the same woman who had left Wellington's headquarters.

"I can't," she said, quietly. Suddenly, Pippa saw her father not as Sir Hew, the British envoy, but as a man who'd been hurt by love.

She'd never understood that before. She did now. Loving William had opened both her heart and her mind. Her world was no longer black and white, correct and incorrect. She now saw the nuances of life and how not releasing the pain of her mother's abandonment had hurt both her and her father.

"I don't want you angry," she said to her father, placing a hand on his arm. "My care and devotion for you is as strong as ever, but William is my husband. I chose him, and I beg you to consider him like a son."

For a moment, she thought her father would soften. In the end, he turned and walked out the door.

Pippa took a step after him and then stopped. She turned to William.

"I'm sorry," he said.

"He doesn't understand yet that a heart can hold love for more than one person. He's shut that part of him off."

"Do you want me to talk to him?" he asked. "I will, for you."

Her William, always so ready to take up a cause. "It would be of little use. I just pray you don't hold this against him. I do want him in my life."

"As he should be."

William made the arrangements for her then. He booked passage for her and Lilly to England and prepared a letter introducing her to his family.

Their parting was the worst moment of Pippa's life. She didn't want to let him go.

She also knew he had to go to battle. It was what a soldier did.

JUST AS WILLIAM had predicted, his family welcomed her with open arms. Pippa and his mother became great friends. Mrs. Duroy was more outspoken than any woman Pippa had ever met, and she adored her.

She also liked his father, brothers, and their wives.

What was interesting was that she discovered that the women in her own family—such as her aunt, Lady Romley--were more caring of her than she had originally imagined. Pippa wondered if her father's distrust had carried over to her, so she didn't see other women as they really were.

One thing she did not like about her new life was making the trip after major battles to the center of York to read the rolls of the dead posted on the Cathedral door. And every time William's name was not on the list, she went into the church and knelt in prayer.

She wrote him every day. He wrote her when he could, and she valued every connection to him.

She also wrote her father at least twice month. There was no response.

It was during this time when books once again became her allies. Reading was not a way to stave off living, but to help blunt the edges. True to his word, William had seen that her library left behind at Wellington's headquarters was sent to her. She hated to think how much transporting them had cost him.

And then one day, William returned. Colonel William Duroy.

Pippa was so proud of him. In a very private service, and with a special license, Pippa and William married in the Church of England. That very night, they conceived their first child.

William had to return to the fight, but he promised he would be home for his son's birth—and he was.

Holding her baby in her arms for the first time, Pippa felt a sense of completeness she had not known could exist. And in that moment, she pitied her mother. The woman who had abandoned her husband and her child had given up so much. Pippa could not, and would never be able to understand her.

Her only sadness was the loss of her father.

Christian Nelson Duroy was christened on the third Sunday of October.

The sky was clear and blue, the wind brisk. The church was filled with the Duroy family, all proud to welcome this newest member to their number.

As the priest began the ceremony, William leaned over and whispered, "Look in the back of the church."

Pippa turned, and there was her father. He looked older, sadder.

And she was glad he was there.

Afterward, father and daughter didn't waste time discussing the past. To Pippa, all that mattered was the present, the here and now. A soldier's wife learned to think that way.

Yes, William would be leaving again. There would be many times she would fear for his life, but now she understood how full and encompassing love was. It defied the simple explanations of poets, and no novelist could ever give it full justice. Not with mere words on a printed page.

No, living life fully was the only way to understand love, and so she loved well.

COLONEL WILLIAM DUROY retired from the military after the Battle of Waterloo. The time had come for him to be a man of peace. He ran for Parliament from Yorkshire and was elected as a representative of the Tory party. He was knighted for his service to his country in 1827. He and his wife, Pippa, enjoyed a long and fruitful marriage. They were the parents of eight children, three sons and five daughters, all of them redheads.

Don't miss
LYON'S BRIDE,
the first book in
Cathy Maxwell's unforgettably romantic new series,
THE CHATTAN CURSE—
On sale NOW
Only from Avon Books

When a Chattan Male falls in love, strike his heart with fire from above . . .

They call him Lord Lyon, proud, determined—and cursed. He is in need of a bride, but if he falls in love, he dies. And so he wants a woman he cannot love. His fervent hope is that by marrying—and having a son—without love, perhaps he can break the curse's chains forever.

Enter beautiful Thea Martin—a duke's headstrong, errant daughter and society's most brilliant matchmaker. Years ago, she and Lyon were inseparable until he disappeared from her life without a word. Now, she is charged with finding Lyon's Bride—a woman he cannot love for a man Thea could love too well.

Or will the power of love be enough to overcome all obstacles?

The Curse

Macnachtan Keep
Scotland, 1632

A MOTHER KNOWS. 'Tis the curse of giving birth.

She feels life enter this world, a knife-sharp pain and one gladly borne for the outcome. She nurtures, protects and prays for her child's safekeeping with every breath she draws . . . and so is it any wonder she would also sense, *know*, the moment that precious life is cut short?

Fenella, the wife of the late Laird Macnachtan, was in the south gallery where the sun was best, plying her needle when terror seized her heart. She looked to her kinswomen, all gathered around for an afternoon chat as was their custom. These were her husband's cousins, his sisters, and her daughters Ilona and Aislin—

"Where's Rose?"

A mother should not have a favorite, but Fenella did.

Her other daughters were merry and bright, but Rose was special. She shared her mother's gift of healing. Fenella had delighted in the realization that the powers of her mother and her *nain*—her grandmother—now flowed through her to her youngest. Rose would be "the one" to receive the Book That Contained All Knowledge.

Of course, Rose's golden beauty was the stuff of legend, and that set her apart as well. The suitors for her hand had formed a line across the land, but there had only been one man for Rose—Charles Chattan of Glenfinnan.

Rose's love for Charles reminded Fenella so much of her younger self, that self who had challenged and won the heart of the handsome Macnachtan. That self who was willful and bold.

But Chattan had proved a faithless lover. He'd hand-fasted himself to Rose and then accepted marriage to another—an Englishwoman from a family with power. *Sassenach* power.

With a jolt, Fenella realized today was Charles and the Englishwoman's wedding day. She should not have forgotten the fact. No wonder Rose had been so quiet this morning and was not here amongst the chatter of women this afternoon. Fenella's worry eased a bit.

Rose had loved Charles hard and well. Her heart hurt, but Fenella would see that Rose *would* recover. Thank the Lord, Macnachtan was not alive to witness the Chattans' dishonoring of his daughter. It had been all Fenella could do to keep her sons from calling Charles out. She refused to spill her family's blood over the traitor.

She could not see Rose's future—her gift failed her when she attempted to discern Fate—but there would be another love for Rose. There must be. The powerful gifts handed through accident of birth from one ancestress to another needed to take seed in Rose's womb. . . .

Suddenly a scream rose from the courtyard, an alarm of shock and grief.

In that instant, Fenella's foreboding gained life.

The other women scrambled to their feet and ran to the window overlooking the stone courtyard. Fenella didn't move. Her whole being centered on one whispered word. *"Rose."*

There were more shouts now. Fenella heard her son Michael call his sister's name, heard weeping, wails of distress and mourning. Her kinswomen at the window threw themselves into shocked grief. They turned, looked at Fenella. Ilona, her face contorted, stumbled toward her mother. Aislin knelt, bowled over in pain.

Fenella set aside her needlework.

She did not want to go to that window.

Tears burned her eyes. She held them back. She didn't weep. Not ever. She'd not shed one tear for Macnachtan's death. Death was part of life . . . that's what *Nain* had said. One didn't grieve for life.

Fenella stood.

It was hard to breathe.

She walked to the window. Ilona held out her arms

and then dropped them, as if knowing she could not stop her mother.

Leaning forward, Fenella looked out upon the courtyard below.

Rose's body was sprawled there, her golden hair mingled with a stream of blood flowing from her head.

Her dear daughter. Her darling, darling daughter.

She'd thrown herself from the tower wall.

She'd taken her own life.

Michael looked up and saw his mother. Tears flowed freely down his face.

He was so like his father—

In that moment, Fenella's legs gave out beneath her. She fell to the cold stone floor.

Nain was wrong. Grief could not be contained. It started as a small flame that grew larger and stronger until it consumed her.

THERE WAS NO doubt Rose of Loch Awe had taken her life because of Charles Chattan's perfidy, no saving her memory from the disgrace of suicide.

Fenella longed for the magic to reverse time and bring her daughter back to life.

For the next three days she poured over her *nain's* book. Certainly in all these receipts and spells for healing, for fortune, for doubts and fears, there must be one to cast off Death.

The handwriting on those yellowed pages was cramped and in many places faded. Fenella had signed the front of the book but not referred to it often, at least not once she'd memorized the cures for fevers and agues that plagued children and concerned mothers.

She'd been surprised to discover Rose had also been reading the book. She'd found where Rose had written the name *Charles* beside a spell to find true love. It called for a rose thorn to be embedded in the wax of a candle and burned on the night of a full moon.

They found a piece of the burned candle, the thorn still intact, its tip charred, beneath Rose's pillow.

Fenella held the wax in the palm of her hand. Slowly, she closed her fingers around it into a fist and set aside mourning.

In its place rose anger.

'Twas said the Chattan kin had run for England. The rest had scattered to other clans. They feared Fenella of the Macnachtan, and well they should. Grief made her mad.

They thought themselves safe. They were not.

There was no sacred ground for a suicide, but Fenella had no need of the church. She ordered a funeral pyre to be built for her daughter along the green banks of Loch Awe directly beneath a stony crag that looked down upon the shore.

On the day of Rose's burial, Fenella stood upon that crag, waiting for the sun to set. She wore the Macnachtan tartan around her shoulders. The evening wind toyed her gray hair held in place by a circlet of gold, gray hair that had once been as fair as Rose's.

At Fenella's signal, her sons set ablaze a ring of bonfires she'd ordered constructed around Rose's pyre. The flames leaped to life.

"Rose." Her name was sweet upon her mother's lips.

Did Chattan think he could hide in London? Did his father believe his son could jilt Rose without penalty? That her life had no meaning?

That Macnachtan honor was a small thing?

"I want him to feel my pain," Fenella whispered.

Ilona and Aislin stood by her side. They nodded.

"He will not escape me," Fenella vowed.

"But he is gone," Ilona said. "He has become a fine lord while we are left to weep."

Feeling the heat of the bonfires. She knew better.

At last the moon was high in the sky. The time was right. *Nain* had said a witch knows when the hour is nigh. Tonight would be a night no one would forget. Ever.

Especially Charles Chattan.

The fires had drawn the curious from all over the kirk. They stood on the shore watching her. Fenella raised her hand. Her clansmen and her kin on the shore below fell silent. Michael picked up the torch and held it ready.

She brought her hand down and her oldest lit his sister's funeral pyre as instructed.

'Twas the ancient ways. There was no priest here, no clergy to call her out—and even if there was, Fenella's power in this moment was too strong to be swayed. It coursed through her. It was the beating of her heart, the pulsing in the blood in her veins, the very fiber of her being.

She stepped to the edge of the rock and stared down

over the burning pyre. The flames licked the skirt of Rose's white burial gown.

"My Rose died of love," she said. She whispered the words but then repeated them with a commanding strength. They carried on the wind and seemed to linger over Loch Awe's moonlit waters. "A woman's lot is hard," she said. "'Tis love that gives us courage, gives us strength. My Rose gave the precious gift of her love to a man unworthy of it."

Heads nodded agreement. There was not a soul around who had not been touched by Rose. They all knew her gift of laughter, her kindness, her willingness to offer what help she could to others.

Fenella reached a hand back. Ilona placed the staff that Fenella had ordered hewn from a yew tree and banded with copper. *"I curse Charles Chattan."*

Raising the staff, Fenella said, "I curse not just Chattan but his line. He betrayed her for a title. He tossed aside handfasted promises for greed. Now let him learn what his duplicity has wrought."

The moon seemed to brighten. The flames on the fires danced higher, and Fenella knew she was being summoned. Danse macabre. All were equal in death.

She spoke, her voice ringing in the night.

"Watchers of the threshold, Watchers of the gate,
open hell and seal Chattan's Fate.
When a Chattan male falls in love,
strike his heart with fire from Above.
Crush his heart, destroy his line;
Only then will justice be mine."

Fenella threw her staff down upon her daughter's funeral pyre. The flames now consumed Rose. Fenella could feel their heat, smell her daughter's scent—and she threw herself off the rock, following her staff to where it lay upon Rose's breast. She grabbed her daughter's burning body and clung fast.

Together they left this world.

SIX MONTHS TO the date after his wedding, Charles Chattan died. His heart stopped. He was sitting at his table, accepting congratulations from his dinner guests over the news his wife was breeding, when he fell face-down onto his plate.

The news of his death shocked many. He was so young. A vital, handsome man with so much to live for. Had he not recently declared to many of his friends that he'd fallen in love with his new wife? How could God cut short his life, especially when he was so happy?

But his marriage was not in vain. Seven months after his death, his wife bore a son to carry on the Chattan name . . . a son who also bore the curse.

Chapter One

London
April 1814

THEA MARTIN'S FIRST thought upon receiving a letter from Sir James Smiley, Esq., renowned solicitor for Persons of Great Importance, was that her brother had hatched a new scheme to chase her out of London.

Her hands shook as she broke the sealing wax. So far, her brother Horace had attempted to bar all doors to her, an effort that had not succeeded, since London loved nothing more than a scandal—and the feud between the mighty duke of Duruset and his disinherited sister was great fodder for gossip.

Horace's next action had been to block all reasonable landlords from letting to her. His machinations came to naught, because Thea was determined. London offered opportunities for her to make a living, something difficult for a penniless widow with children to do on her own elsewhere. This had been her home before she'd run away to marry Boyd Martin, and it offered the only hope for her small family's future.

Thea had found a tiny set of rooms for let in a shabby building in a less-than-respectable neighborhood. It meant she would keep her boys in all day instead of giving them a garden for play, but it was a start, and that had been what Thea had needed—a new beginning.

Using the connections she'd made during her debutante years, she'd set about using the only skill she knew, matchmaking. She knew the ways of the *ton*, she knew marriage, and she understood the desperation of parents. She also knew how to be discreet.

And if her brother was not pleased? Well, she was already disowned. What more could he do?

Thea feared she'd discover the answer to that last question in Sir James's letter.

"What is it, Mother?" Jonathan asked. He was a bright, towheaded seven-year-old who wanted to be her protector. His brother, five-year-old Christopher, stood by his side, his little forehead wrinkled in concern. Their small family didn't receive letters often.

"I will tell you in a moment," Thea murmured. "Are you waiting for my reply?" she asked the messenger, who still lingered in the hall with a distasteful sniff at his surroundings.

"Yes, ma'am. I've been ordered to return with your reply."

Thea forced herself to focus on Sir James's slanting handwriting. He wanted to see her on "a matter of Some Importance." He mentioned he was the uncle of Peter Goodfellow, for whom she had "performed a service that was nothing short of a Miracle" and that he hoped she'd be willing to "assist Someone again facing the same Situation."

Peter Goodfellow had been one of Thea's matchmaking challenges. He was as tall as he was wide, had a squint, liked to pick at his face, and had a distressing tendency to burp. She'd found a wife for him, but it had not been an easy task. His family's handsome commission had compensated for the difficulty. Thea wondered if this request could mean another large commission.

Oh, were it to be so. She'd hidden most of the Goodfellow commission in her "Future Box," the small, wooden money chest kept under the floorboard beneath her bed. Her goal was to see that both her sons received a gentleman's education. Jonathan had an interview in a month's time with the headmaster of Westminster School, a prestigious day school that would offer him the opportunity to meet boys from the right sort of families, families far different from those living in their present neighborhood.

"Sir James wished to know if you could meet with him today at half past two," the messenger said politely.

"Half past two?" Thea consulted the clock on the

mantel over the hearth. It had been Boyd's mother's and was the nicest thing she owned. It was already one. "Yes, of course I can." She reached for her reticule and pulled out a coin to tip the man.

The messenger smiled as he saw her open her purse, a smile that turned brittle at the small amount she placed in his palm. She knew what he was thinking, but she didn't care. She must watch every penny.

"I shall return to him with your acceptance." The messenger bowed and was on his way.

Thea shut the door. For a second, she allowed herself a moment's relief over the letter not being from her brother—and then she danced a little jig. Christopher started dancing with her, his worry giving way to a huge smile.

"What was in the letter, Mother?" Jonathan asked, too dignified to join in their little party.

She knelt down to the level of her two handsome sons. "A chance to earn the money we need for your school fees." She wrapped her arms around them and gave them both a big hug. "I was so worried, but God does provide." Yes, yes, yes. She'd been living on what God provided ever since Boyd had abandoned them in Manchester right after Christopher was born.

"Do I still have the interview with the school next month?" Jonathan asked.

"Yes," Thea said, "and you shall do very well. Westminster will be happy to have you. But first, I must see Sir James." She was on her feet in a blink, her mind a flurry of activity.

She needed someone to watch her sons while she was

out. She ran up the hallway stairs to Mrs. Hadley's door. Mrs. Gray, Mrs. Hadley's sister by marriage, answered. She'd only arrived last week, and Thea didn't know very much about her except that her late husband had been a country vicar. She was a petite woman with a comfortable bosom and sad brown eyes.

"I am looking for Mrs. Hadley," Thea said.

"Oh, she is off to care for my brother at the hospital," Mrs. Gray replied. "You know how it is in those places. If your family doesn't see to your care, you can rot." Mr. Hadley suffered from consumption. Thea had been relieved when he'd been taken to the London Hospital, away from her boys, with his coughing and hacking.

"This is sad news," Thea said. "I wanted to ask her to watch my sons while I ran an errand. Mrs. Hadley is usually home by now."

"I don't know what has been keeping her, but if it is help you need, I'll watch your boys for you," Mrs. Gray volunteered.

Thea's first instinct was to refuse the kind offer. She hated leaving her sons alone at any time and was very particular about whom she asked for help.

However, this was a special circumstance.

"Are you certain it wouldn't be a bother?" Thea asked. "I dislike imposing."

"No trouble at all. I've seen your lads walking with you. They seem to be good boys."

She had such a soft, melodic voice and grandmotherly way—and Thea really didn't have another choice. Not on such short notice.

"Thank you," Thea said, meaning the words. "I must change my dress, but if you could come down in ten minutes?"

"Of course I will."

Thea didn't waste another moment. She flew down the stairs, changed her into her best dress, a cambric gown in a brown with a reddish tint, then donned a very plain poke bonnet and dark green pelisse. Within ten minutes, convinced she looked every inch the part of a sensible matchmaker, Thea set off for Sir James's offices on Beatty Street.

THEA ACTUALLY ARRIVED a few minutes early for the interview.

The law offices of Sir James Smiley, Esq., consisted of two rooms. Sir James's clerk sat at a desk in the first room. At her entrance, he jumped to his feet. He was all of seventeen, with a slender frame and straight blonde hair parted to one side. He pushed his spectacles up his nose. "Mrs. Martin? Sir James is waiting for you."

Thea always used her married name. She never even thought of herself as Lady Thea, which had really been nothing more than a courtesy title, since she was the daughter of a duke. In truth, a true lady would never style herself above her husband, and at this point in her life, Thea was concerned about what was honest and real over "courtesy." After all, her ducal father had disowned her, and, as Mrs. Martin, she was determined to stand on her own two feet . . . no matter how wobbly she felt doing so at times.

"I hope I'm not too late?" Thea said, nerves making her sound a bit breathless.

"You are right on time," the clerk assured her. "One moment, please." He crossed to the room's other door, gave a knock and opened it. "Sir James, Mrs. Martin has arrived."

"Send her in, send her in," a hearty male voice ordered.

The secretary held open the door. "Mrs. Martin," he announced, ushering her forward with a small sweep of his hand.

Her heart pounding in her ears, Thea crossed into the other room.

Sir James's book-lined office was the typical sort one would expect from a solicitor. The desk was huge and covered with neatly stacked papers, the ink-and-quill stand was solid silver, and there was a side table for the wig stand that held the curled peruke of his profession. Two comfortable wooden chairs were arranged in front of the desk.

"Come in, come in," Sir James said in greeting as he walked around the desk to welcome her.

He was a robust man with flinty blue eyes, a hawkish nose and an air that proclaimed him no one's fool. "I've heard much about you, Mrs. Martin, and it is a pleasure to make your acquaintance. Please, have a chair."

Thea sat on the edge of the offered chair, holding her

reticule in her lap with both gloved hands. Sir James took his seat behind his desk.

He smiled at her.

She smiled back, very nervous.

"I suppose you are wondering why I requested this interview?" he asked.

"You mentioned my assistance to Mr. Goodfellow," she murmured.

"I'm his uncle, and only one as familiar as I was with the situation can truly appreciate the miracle you wrought. All of us in the family adore his wife, Emma. How you managed to convince her to marry him is beyond our understanding, but we are thankful you did. In fact, his mother, my sister, has suggested I should think about seeking your services. She claims I'm too old to continue bachelor ways, but I am not ready to hand over my freedom yet. By the way, did you hear that Peter and his wife are expecting their first child?" Sir James asked. "One can hope the child looks more like Emma than Peter." He paused before adding thoughtfully, "You know, Emma seems to love him. She sees the better qualities in him."

And finding a suitable husband without the aid of even a modest dowry meant Emma had little choice in husbands Thea could have added, but didn't. "How wonderful for them."

"Yes, and when one of my clients mentioned he wished to find a wife to meet his most unusual specifications, I thought of you."

"Thank you," Thea said. She prayed this wasn't going

to be a task as difficult as Peter Goodfellow had been. "But exactly what is the gentleman looking for in a wife?"

Instead of answering, the lawyer straightened in his chair, listening.

Male voices came from the other room, one the clerk's and the other a deep, well-modulated tone. Sir James smiled. "I'll let him tell you himself. I believe you will be pleased. He won't be as challenging a case as my nephew." He rose and crossed the room, throwing open the door. "My lord," he said in greeting. "Good of you to join us."

"She's here?" his lordship said.

Thea came to her feet. She caught a glimpse of the gentleman but could not see his face from this angle. She had the impression he was taller than Sir James, and that was good. Women liked tall men.

"Yes, she is, and very interested in meeting you," Sir James said.

"I don't know," the gentleman said, doubt filling his voice.

"Speak to her. See what you think," Sir James said. He stepped aside to let the gentleman enter the room first.

Thea caught her breath in anticipation, silently praying this man was not an unfortunate-looking soul like Peter Goodfellow. After all, there was *usually* something wrong with all of her charges, else they wouldn't need her guidance—

Her breath left her with a small exclamation of surprise.

He wasn't her *usual* charge.

This man was everything a young lord should be.

He was tall, taller than most, with square shoulders and no sign of belly bulge or flabby calves. Strong legs were encased in buff-colored breeches and shining, tall black boots. He was handsome. Slashing black brows, a resolute jaw, blue eyes that seemed to look right into a person. The material of his bottle green jacket was of the finest wool and molded to his shoulders in such a way that she knew he did not need padding.

Indeed, there was so much masculine energy about him that most women would find it hard to breathe, let alone think, in his presence. Thea was no exception. Her mind had come to an abrupt halt. She couldn't think, couldn't speak, couldn't do anything but stare, and not out of admiration . . . but from the shock of recognition.

Before her stood the wealthy, reclusive Neal Chattan, Lord Lyon—the most eligible bachelor in society, and a man who had once been her closest confidant until he'd rudely rejected her friendship.

"Mrs. Martin," Sir James said with the eagerness of someone very pleased with himself, "this is Lord Lyon." He shut the door behind him and came into the room. "My lord, may I present to you Mrs. Martin, the matchmaker I've suggested you enlist."

Neal appeared to be having his own bout of mind-numbing recollection. He didn't react to Sir James's introduction but stared at Thea with an unnerving intensity.

Or, perhaps, age had made his expression intense. She wouldn't know. Their paths hadn't crossed in close to fourteen years.

But he was here before her now.

She straightened her back and lifted her chin, keeping both hands on her reticule for balance, for support. "My lord." She almost choked on the words. She'd heard his father had died several years ago, knew that he'd ascended to the title.

"*Mrs.* Martin?" He moved a step away, as if uncertain.

His movement allowed her to take two paces opposite his. "I married," she said.

"Apparently."

Sir James looked at Thea, looked at Lord Lyon, and then back at her. The welcoming smile left his face, replaced by uncertainty. "Do you two know each other?"

"Barely," Thea replied crisply even as Lord Lyon barked, "Hardly."

The twin words lingered in the air, followed by a beat of heavy silence, and Thea couldn't help but remember their childhood days together, back when her father had always banished his children to the countryside, where the favored sons had been encouraged to hunt and fish, and the girls had been left to sew samplers. Thea had escaped the house back then and come across Neal, who'd been just as lonely as herself.

Lord Lyon must have been thinking along the same lines. "I knew her when she was Lady Thea," he told Sir James. There was an accusatory tone to his voice that Thea did not like.

Sir James dismissed this bit of information with a wave of his hand. "Yes, yes, we all know she is the duke of Duruset's daughter. You needn't worry about the current Duruset's opinion, my lord. His father disowned her when she married. The current duke has stated publicly he won't have anything to do with her."

Lord Lyon frowned. "Is that true?" he demanded of Thea.

She was not pleased to have her business bandied about, yet she was also proudly defiant. "It must be," she said. "Sir James wrote the letter from my father cutting me off."

"Bad bit of business it was," Sir James said, moving around his desk to his chair. "Never enjoy those sorts of things, and I admit I've been doing what I can to help her out. She's widowed now. The marriage is done, but she is developing a very respectable reputation at putting the right sort of people together. She helped immeasurably with Peter, and you know we fretted of ever marrying him off. Considering your unusual desires for a wife, you'd be wise to listen to her."

"Perhaps his lordship would not care to work with me," Thea suggested stiffly.

"Perhaps," Sir James echoed. He stood behind his desk now, his fingers resting on its polished surface. "Will you sit down and discuss the matter with her, Lyon? Or shall I toss her out?" He said this last with the familiarity of one who knew his customer.

Lord Lyon shifted his weight as if in indecision, and then he shrugged. "Very well, she may try. I suppose it doesn't matter who I use as long as she is effective."

"I believe you will be pleased," Sir James said. He smiled. "Perhaps someday I shall use her myself. Like you, I must marry sooner or later. Will you sit, Mrs. Martin?"

Thea had the urge to run from the room, but then she thought of her sons, of her looming plans for Jonathan's education. Lyon was rich. "I shall stay, but it will cost you a pretty penny, my lord," she said, wanting to give him a bit of his own arrogance back. "My services are not inexpensive."

"I can't imagine they would be," Lord Lyon replied. "In fact, if you find the wife I am looking for, I'll triple whatever your commission is."

Thea sat.

Lord Lyon took his seat.

"Now isn't this better?" Sir James said brightly, taking his own chair.

Thea forced a smile. Neal remained stony-faced.

She decided to really tweak Lyon's nose and take charge. "Sir James said you have particular qualities you are looking for in a wife. Please tell me what they are?"

He shifted in his chair, crossed his arms and his legs, not looking at her.

"Do you wish her to have blonde hair?" Thea queried in a pert, businesslike voice—one that she knew would needle him. "Or a brunette? Do you like voluptuous women? Or perhaps a more slender version?"

Lord Lyon looked to Sir James. "This is uncomfortable."

"They are reasonable questions, Lyon," Sir James said. "If she is to search for a wife for you, then she must know."

"Or," Thea said, "you could head out on the Marriage Mart and look for yourself." The "Marriage Mart" was the name given to the round of social parties and engagements during the season when Parliament was in session. Many a match had been made at these events.

"I don't want to do that," he said, still not making eye contact with her.

A memory came to her of the two of them sitting on the same rock beside a running stream, their secret place. She'd been what? Fourteen? He must have been sixteen. She saw them, their heads together, laughing, drawing courage from each other. Their friendship had helped make her world sane, and then the next day, she'd escaped to meet him again as they had done every morning for the past month or more, and he hadn't been there. She'd visited the site every day for the rest of her summer, and he'd never showed again.

No warning, no explanation . . . and then, in the fall, she'd heard that he'd left for school and she'd stopped searching for him. She'd not seen him again until this moment.

"Then I shall need to know what you are looking for if I am to sift through the large number of women who would be very pleased to marry a wealthy, well-respected nobleman." She heard herself sounding like a society matron planning a party. She liked the tone. It was distant and didn't convey the turbulence of her own emotions.

His jaw hardened.

When he didn't speak, Sir James prompted him once again. "Lyon, what are you looking for in a wife?"

His lordship stirred himself then to sit up. He answered, still addressing himself to Sir James, his voice low, almost inaudible. "Good family."

How original, Thea wanted to say. Instead, she said, "Absolutely. And other qualities?"

There was a beat of silence. Thea felt her disdain for this man growing. After the confidences they had shared, how could he sit beside her as if they were strangers? How could he be so bloody cold?

"I don't want a cold woman," he said, as if he'd divined her thoughts. "My mother was cold. Some say I am as well."

But he didn't used to be. A wave of sadness swept away her disdain.

"Good with children," he continued. "Our children must be her priority."

Something that hadn't been true about his mother.

Thea resisted the urge to place a comforting hand upon his arm. If Neal hadn't valued their friendship, he certainly wouldn't want her pity now.

"And she must be someone I cannot like," he said. "Admired by others . . . but *I must not like her.*"

Warm thoughts of him vanished from Thea's mind. "You don't want to 'like' the woman who will be your wife?"

At last he faced her, his features set. *"No."*

"My lord, that is a ludicrous, irresponsible position." The words had just burst out of her, carried by her previous disappointments in him.

Apparently, few talked to Lord Lyon in such a direct manner. Sir James's mouth dropped open.

His lordship sat up even taller. "I find it very responsible."

"Then you are deceiving yourself," Thea said. She'd gone this far, she might as well go further. "Not all marriages can be built on love, but those are the best. At the very least there should be the compatibility of admiration and respect. Of *liking* the person you take a vow before God to cherish and honor."

"That is your opinion. It is not mine."

Thea looked into his eyes and saw a stranger. "Whatever happened to that boy I once knew who believed in friendship?" she said. "That lad whose confidences I valued and whose opinion I trusted?"

"Let us take a moment to consider our words," Sir James advised, as if wishing to avert a disaster.

"I can't help you arrange such a marriage as this," Thea went on, ignoring the lawyer. "Knowing what I do of you, it would not be right."

"You know nothing of me," Lord Lyon countered.

"I beg to differ, my lord. I may know more of you than you know of yourself."

"And what would that be?" he challenged.

Thea sat back, realizing she was now on very sensitive ground. How well *did* she know him? How much *had* he changed?

Certainly she wasn't the same person she'd been during those long-ago summer days.

But one thing was still clear in her mind—she believed in love.

The acknowledgement startled her. After all that Boyd, her father, her family had put her through, she still believed.

It isn't often one is struck with self-knowledge, and every time it is surprising. Suddenly, she realized why she'd set herself up as a matchmaker. She wanted to right wrongs, to guide others away from the disastrous decisions she'd made in her own life.

She softened her voice. "My lord, marriage is a difficult endeavor. I'm not saying you must love your wife, but you must like her. Otherwise you will be saddling yourself to a cold, uncompromising life." The sort of life his parents had had all those years ago.

The sort of life she remembered him vowing never to live.

Her change in tone worked. The fury in his eyes died, replaced by hopelessness. "You don't understand."

"Then explain to me," she said.

"I'm cursed."

Thea blinked. Uncertain if he was being dramatic or factual. "Cursed?"

"Yes," he said with complete seriousness. "And my only hope of survival is to marry someone I don't like, that I will *never* be able to abide. It will call for a very special woman. I don't want someone I would detest. There is a difference between not liking and detesting."

Thea glanced at Sir James to see if he thought his lordship was spouting nonsense. He nodded his head as if agreeing with Lord Lyon.

"You believe him cursed as well?" Thea challenged the solicitor.

Sir James shrugged. "There is evidence to suggest it."

For a second, Thea wondered if she had wandered into

a world of nonsense—and then her mind seized upon another possibility. A sinister one.

"Is my brother behind this?" she demanded.

Both Lord Lyon and Sir James acted perplexed at her accusation, but she was on to the game now. This was the only explanation that made sense. She stood. "Oh, this was very clever of him. I know Horace is not happy that I remain independent and even dare to go so far as to work for my living. But this?" She shook her head. "You should be ashamed of yourself, Sir James. And you, Lord Lyon. What a faithless friend you are. Apparently your title has destroyed whatever was good inside of you."

"I beg your pardon?" Lord Lyon said. He'd risen when she had and now pretended to be clueless in the face of her accusation.

She moved toward the door. Her excitement over a healthy commission had turned to disappointment.

Sir James came around the desk toward her. "Mrs. Martin, please, I don't know what we said to upset you—"

She cut him off by whirling around, her outstretched hand a warning that she did not want him to come closer. "*Enough*. I can't believe I wasted a half shilling on the two of you. Here you are giving in to my brother's schemes, and for what? A payment, Sir James? Some sort of cloakroom political deal in the House of Lords, Lord Lyon? Oh, yes, I know how the duke works. He's always hatching new alliances for his own benefit. But I once thought you the closest of friends, and to my great dismay, you have grown into a man much like your parents—cold, distant, everything you said you wouldn't be. *Curses,*" she said, biting out the word as if it had been an epithet. "Did you really believe I would be so gullible. Well, return to my brother and tell him no one believes in curses in this day and age. Not even his sister, the one he refuses to acknowledge." With that pronouncement, she opened the door and sailed out of the room.

"Thea, *come back here*," Neal ordered.

Her response was to keep walking.

And don't miss the second book in
THE CHATTAN CURSE series,
THE SCOTTISH WITCH,
Coming in November 2012!

Letters from Pie Town

LYNNE HINTON

POSTED ANNOUNCEMENT

To All Citizens of Pie Town, New Mexico!

Raymond Twinhorse, son of Frank Twinhorse, is a native son of Catron County, born of the Navajo Nation, a lifetime citizen of Pie Town, and now a soldier in need of our attention. Raymond was recently injured in Afghanistan, where he serves as a soldier in the US Army. He has been taken to the military hospital in Germany, where he is receiving the care he needs for his injuries. As a means of encouragement and good wishes, his friends are putting together a "Get Well Parcel" to include letters, small tokens of appreciation, and pictures to send to him. Please take this opportunity to write Raymond and let him know how much we love him!

Oris Whitsett and his daughter, Malene, are in charge of gathering the letters. Father George at Holy Family Church will be accepting any gifts you want to send. Francine Mueller, chief baker at Fred and Bea's diner, will be collecting the money to help pay the shipping costs for this Hometown Hero Goodie Box. Trina Lockhart is in charge of this Pie Town Project so all questions and concerns can be handled by her. Stop by Frank's Garage to find her!

Even though we are a small town, a little place, mostly unknown to others across the state and across the country, let's show our hero that we are big in pride! Just as we have rallied together in the past to take care of each other, let us rally together now and come to the aid of our dearly beloved, Raymond Twinhorse. We are a beautiful village of settlers descended from homesteaders, conquistadors, and Native Americans. We are the hometown of heroes! We are the village of generous hearts! We are the community of those who care! Let us not forget, let us not allow Raymond to forget . . . . We are his family! We are Pie Town!

Dear Raymond,

I hereby certify that this letter is written by my own hand without coercion or unsolicited counsel. My name is Oris Whitsett, and I am of sound mind and fair judgment.

I apologize, Raymond, this was first started as a new draft of my will which I never completed but I don't have much paper for letter writing so I've just got to use what's on hand.

Trina said you liked getting letters. She told us to write you and that she would put all the greetings together and send a big package to the hospital. I even heard that Francine was looking to bake you something special, although I think shipping a pie to Europe might be a bit more messy than she figures. Unless she sends you a pecan pie. Francine's pecan pies get hard as a rock when they've been sitting for more than a day. I suppose if that's what comes with the letters, you could use it as a weapon, seeing how you're still in a military hospital and could possibly be an enemy target.

Trina gave us instructions about what we should say in our letters, asked us to be upbeat and encouraging, give some news about Pie Town and what is going on here since you left. She even has some notion that the mail arrives at your hospital in the afternoon and hopes that upon receiving our package you'll be able to enjoy all these missives, cards, and desserts, when the sun is bright and you're finished with all your doctor's visits and the daily therapy; and as you are left with a lonesome hour or so before dinner you will be heartened by all the well-wishes from your hometown.

Personally, I like to read my mail in the morning along with the newspaper, but of course, our mail doesn't run any more until after lunch since Thelma Gilbert started delivering for all of the residents of Quemado, Datil, and Pie Town. She claims there were budget cuts and they fired the other county carriers. I tried complaining to the Post Office General that the village of Pie Town needed its own post office and letter carrier but like most of the complaints I lodge against our government, I didn't hear no reply.

Frank told us at the diner yesterday that you were sent from Afghanistan over to Germany where you're facing a few operations and that you'll be back stateside in a few weeks or so. He said he hears from your doctors every couple of days and that you're coming along real good. He was informed that your leg is pretty banged up but that your vital organs are strong and your head is clear. He was mighty worried about you when we first found out about the accident over there, closed the garage and everything. It was the middle of the week when he got the call and he told Trina that he was going out to walk the trails and that he'd return soon enough. A few hours after he left we had a real bad snow storm and everybody got some kind of worried about him. I told them all that Navajos know a whole lot more about surviving the elements than us settlers but they were still worried, sent out a few men to try and find him. Then three days later, he just showed up at the garage working on Christine's brakes without a word of where he had been or how he was. You know your dad has his ways.

Before I go on I need to say that I'm not much for writing down things to other folks. I make grocery lists, pay my bills by check, keep a diary of money spent, money earned, a good record of my mileage on the Buick, revise my will every couple of months or so; but I can't recall writing a letter to anyone except for maybe some school project in English class. Miss Dubois was a French lady, came over to the states with her sister who married a soldier during the last world war. She moved out here to Catron County in the late forties, was hard on our little band of students but I learned more from her than anybody else in my eight years of schooling. I believe she had us write letters once or twice, to the President of the United States, the governor over in Santa Fe, and seems like we had to write a letter to someone we admired. I can't recall who I chose for that assignment, but now that

I think about it, it was probably Miss Dubois because I do remember she was easy on the eyes and I was a little taken with her accent. But anyway, all I'm saying is that I not completely sure how this will fare since I don't have much experience in this kind of thing. Usually, if I'm writing a letter, I'm complaining about something, however, since I know you're trying to think on more pleasant matters, I'll try to think of some news to write to you other than how I miss getting my mail and paper at the same time and how the Forest Ranger over at the El Malpais Recreation Area keeps hard liquor in his truck. I saw the bottle for myself when it rolled out from under the driver's seat when he came into town for lunch.

Things in Pie Town haven't changed much since you left for the army. My daughter, Malene, remarried her first husband, Roger, which doesn't make a bit of sense to me. I never understood why they divorced in the first place and then why they would ever bother to go back through the trouble of marrying up again. But that's their concern.

The church was rebuilt after the fire and though I'm still mad about changing the time of Saturday Mass, I did help put up a few walls, filled in the sidewalk with cement, and helped Bernie King level the parking lot. It was, after all, what Alex wanted for the town and Lord knows, I did anything for that great-grandson of mine when he was living and wasn't about to stop after he died. He wanted that church rebuilt more than anything and no matter what I thought about the church and that new priest I couldn't see his pleasures denied. I still miss him as much as I miss my beloved Alice, but that's not anything to write to you about.

My Buick's running good. Got it a few months ago and I think the trunk is even bigger than last year's model. Frank just tuned it up and rotated the tires and I don't mean to talk bad about your father but he charged me way more than they would have at the dealer in Albuquerque. I try to be neighborly and give him my business but you wouldn't even know he notices my generosity by the amounts he charges. Maybe when you get home you can man the office and talk him into coming down on his pricing.

Trina does well at the garage. In the little bit of time she's been working there, she's learned a lot about engines and such. She can change a timing belt, flush out a radiator, switch out the brakes and replace the muffler without any help from Frank. You've picked a fine mate in her, I tell you. I don't know if she can cook but I guarantee you this much, you'll never have to pay for another oil change. She's swift and hardworking and I think she's quite sweet on you, talks about you every time I see you, seems to care a great deal about what happens to you. That counts for a lot, let me tell you. I miss Alice, my wife, more than anything because I always knew she loved me, cared for me. It's the most tender part of life, having a companion, so I'm happy you and Trina found each other.

We still got a lot of winter left and the weatherman said we'll get more snow this weekend. I'm thinking about asking Frank to put chains on my tires but Malene keeps telling me I got nowhere to go anyway. But just let there be some emergency around here and my Buick will be the only car up and running in this whole county. Roger's squad car is so old I won't be surprised if he doesn't go on some sheriff's call and have to be towed out. I keep telling him he needs a new vehicle but he claims the county can't afford it. Maybe now that I'm writing this to you, I will have gotten the hang of letter writing and I'll ask him if he wants me to write to the state and request more funds for the sheriff's department.

Well, that's about all I can think of to tell you right now. I suppose if Miss Dubois was grading, she'd probably say I needed to spend a little more time on my spelling and grammar. I reckon I'll just take my chances with what I got and hope you'll overlook the errors.

We're proud of you, Raymond, for signing up in the army when there was a war going on, for fighting for these United States of America, helping us keep our many freedoms, showing honor and bravery in your service on the battlefield. You know my Lawrence has made a career in the military, fought in both Gulf Wars, served as an instructor overseas and now back here in the states but I want you to know that I feel as much pride in your service as I do my own son's.

We got a fine picture of you on the wall at the diner and everybody here in Pie Town wants you to get well and come back home. We look forward to giving you a hero's welcome, serving you some decent pie, and making sure you know just how much we appreciate all you have done.

Maybe when you get out of the hospital, come home

to Catron County, and wear that nice soldier uniform, you can speak to the General of the Post Office and get my mail back running at a decent time. You take care now and hurry home.

Your friend,
Oris Whitsett

Dear Raymond,

Enclosed in this package that Trina is putting together is a pecan pie I made this morning. It has chocolate and lots of butter and brown sugar and of course,
pecans. Frank said you didn't care for coconut so I left
out that ingredient and added half a cup more of the
nuts. I thought the pecan pie would ship better than the
meringue or fruit ones; and it should stay fresh since we
serve it a couple of days past the bake day at the diner and
nobody seems to notice.

I'm not sure if you heard that I now officially bake
pies at the diner for Fred and Bea. You know, they used
to serve just brownies, maybe a pound cake once in a
while, but they've never been known for their desserts. I
started making pies last year just before the festival, won
the grand prize at the bake off, and took a class later that
season at the community college on creating tasty des-

serts. I like fixing the pies and have even come up with a few recipes on my own. I just find one I like and add a little something else or take out an ingredient I don't care for, replace it with something different, kind of like the extra nuts for the coconut in your pecan one.

Don Martinez from over at the steakhouse in Socorro drove all the way out to Pie Town last summer just to taste my banana cream. I heard it mentioned that he would like me to come down there and make the desserts for his restaurant but I think I'll just stay where I am. Fred and Bea pay me a little more than when I was waitressing and when I get orders from customers at the diner, I am given the full amount received. We charge twenty-five dollars for a pie; so I can do real well when it's a holiday season or somebody is hosting a family reunion. It's a nice arrangement and I don't have to drive so far to work.

When we heard about your accident, the bomb that blew up your army jeep, we all stopped what we were doing and we said a prayer, right then and there. Fred and Bea closed the diner early and then we all gathered at the church and said more prayers. I don't go to Holy Family Church since I'm not Catholic, but that evening everybody in the whole town showed up. Even Oris came and he hasn't been to church since they dedicated the building. He drove his Buick, of course, and even brought Fedora Snow, his neighbor from across the street, although he did make her sit in the back.

Father George read a few passages of scripture. Roger sang a hymn. We lit candles and we prayed. Out loud.

Everybody taking a turn asking God to heal you, to let everything be alright, to bring you back home to us.

Your dad wasn't there and we prayed for him too. Everybody knew he took the news real hard. Walked out of his garage and just went up into the hills. Stayed up there three days in the worst storm we've had all winter. Bernie took his truck up there to find him, but he said he never smelled a wisp of smoke or saw a single print in the snow and you know, Bernie's pretty good at tracking.

Of course, Frank came back and even though he doesn't talk much about it, he seems like he's doing better now that we know you're out of Afghanistan, in the hospital in Germany, and doing okay. He's back to work, at least, which is good for Pie Town because most everybody needs help putting chains on their tires.

Trina said that I should tell you about me and Mr. King, Bernie. I know you worked some for him on his ranch when you were younger. She said that you would like to hear that we started dating because she hadn't actually told you yet since it just became official only a few weeks ago. She says that, but I figure she already let the cat out of the bag because it was her pushing that really got us together. Bernie, Mr. King, is an old bachelor, set in his ways; and truth be told, I never thought he'd ask me out. But you know Trina. She said something to him and the next thing I know, I'm riding with him over to Silver City for dinner and a movie. It was some crazy western cowboy show that had aliens in it. That Harrison Ford was the main cowboy and Bernie knew I liked him in those Indiana Jones movies so he found out when this new film was showing at the cinema and asked me to join him. He came to the diner to ask and when I looked over at Trina, who was there eating lunch, she just grinned from ear to ear. I figure she knew what he was asking before I did.

Trina's been a good friend to me in the last year. I know it seems strange, us being so different in ages, me being old enough to be her mother or even grandmother, but she's just so easy to talk to, so down to earth, truthful. I find her to be a person of great courage and strength. She's quite a gal, but I guess that's news you already know, right?

She tells me about how you've been talking on the computer, how you write letters, send messages on that thing called Placebook or something like that. Maybe she wouldn't want me to say this, but Raymond, the girl lights up like a Christmas tree when your name is mentioned. I don't know how you can see each other on that little computer screen or how you can have a conversation of any real value when you're so far away, but she sure seems like she knows you as good or better than those of us who watched you grow up. And if my friend is happy, then I'm happy too. Besides I told her this and I'll tell you the same thing, she couldn't find a better man anywhere.

I tell her about how you were as a boy, so quiet, like your dad, so interested in how things work. Always reading and learning. As I recall, you were also a sucker for any old stray dog or cat that wandered through town. I remember when you were about ten years old and you found a rabbit near my house. You wrapped it up in your shirt and brought it to the front door. You were so gentle with that little thing. You asked me if it was mine and when I explained I didn't keep rabbits, you said it hurt his leg and you wanted to tend to it and asked me if it was okay if you took him home. I asked Frank about that rabbit a number of years later and he told me how you fed it and cared for it and then let it out at Bernie's ranch. When I mentioned it to Bernie a couple of months ago, he told me that he would see that old rabbit near his back shed for years. He said it hung around there longer than some of the barn cats. He claimed you were still feeding it all those months you worked out there as a teenager. All my life living out in the country I haven't ever heard of a rabbit living longer than a couple of months, maybe a year, especially out here. With all the coyotes and hawks and owls, a rabbit is lucky to make it through one mating season.

Maybe when you get home, you and Trina, the baby, and me and Bernie can ride over to Grants for a nice dinner or even down to Albuquerque for a ball game or a trip to the shopping mall or something. I know we're old but it would still be nice to spend some time with the three of you. I guess Trina has showed you pictures of Alexandria, maybe held her up to that computer camera for you to see. She's growing like a weed and jabbers on about as much as her mamma. She's going to be a talker. But she's so cute you just want to eat her up with a spoon.

We love you, Raymond. We think of you every day, light church candles, say our prayers. We're looking after Trina and your father and we want you to come home soon. Bernie sends his greetings. He's not one for writing down sentiments but he wanted me to make sure you know that he cares for you and misses you a whole lot. He says his farm wasn't ever as well-tended as it was when you were there in those spring and summer seasons you helped him out. He never found a grown man as dedicated, honest, and as hardworking as you were and you weren't even old enough to drive. He calls you the hero of Pie Town.

When you get back home to Catron County, I'll give you the recipe for the pecan pie and I'll make you whatever dessert you like best. Trina said you like the lemon bars they serve in the army so I'll start working on a special lemon pie recipe this week.

Hurry home.

Love,

Francine Mueller

Dear Raymond,

I send you all manner of blessings and prayers of healing with this letter. As the pastor of your home church
here at Holy Family, I am writing to let you know that
we lift you up in the merciful arms of God and keep you
in our hearts and minds every day. I think the idea that
Trina had of sending you a parcel of well-wishes is a good
one and I am happy to include a handmade rosary from
the Brothers at the Norbertine Hermitage Center in Albuquerque and a prayer book from the diocese office in
Gallup. I have also included drawings from the children
in the Sunday School class at Holy Family who are sending their prayers and greetings to you as well. I especially
like Little Tillie Romero's drawing of the church, a yellow
ribbon wrapped around the entire building and a star
overhead, bright and shining above it. She said it is the
same star that brought the wise men to Bethlehem and if

it was able to bring them to the baby Jesus, it is strong and bright enough to bring you home.

It's been a few months since we talked about the Epiphany event and the arrival of the wise men to the stable where our Savior was born, but I guess she finds great comfort in the story and still remembers the long journey across the desert that the Magi made and is considering the deserts of Afghanistan that you have traveled across while making your return to Pie Town. She is also the one who created the bracelet made from wildflowers that is likely to wilt before completing its arrival. I didn't have the heart to tell her that her beautiful piece of jewelry, picked with great care from across the road from her house and braided together, would probably not withstand the time and rigors involved in shipping. When you find the small plastic bag with shriveled stems and petals, just know it comes with great thought and love from Tillie.

I understand that you don't really know me and that you grew up under the care of Father Joseph here at Holy Family Church. He was a good man and a favorable and popular priest. At the time of his death, all of the members of the church attended his funeral held in Quemado six months ago. He was faithful until the very end and I know will be greeted in Heaven by the saints and angels celebrating his good service and his life of dedication. I know he would want me to send his love and care for you as well.

Of course, you have probably already heard the story of my arrival to Pie Town since I got here the very same day as Trina. In fact, as I'm sure she has told you, we drove into town together. She was quite a handful on that ride. Perhaps she mentioned to you that I was not a very experienced driver and I was unsure of where the parish was, what time I was anticipated, and what folks would be expecting in their new priest. With all these concerns, let me just say that I was not at all inclined to offer a ride to a young teenager from Texas who was arriving in Catron County with about as much information about Pie Town as I had. Even though I worked quite diligently to try and put a distance between Trina and me both in the minds of my parishioners and in any kind of relationship she thought we might have, I now recognize quite clearly my pride, arrogance, and lack of charity and count our friendship as one of my greatest gifts as a priest and as a human being. She has shown more strength of character and gentleness of spirit in the couple of years we have known each other than I could possibly ever demonstrate in a lifetime.

She is a wonderful mother even though she doubts her skills. She loves Alexandria and is very careful to attend to the little girl's needs and desires. She is a loyal employee at the garage with your dad, knows more about an engine than I ever will; and she has become a faithful friend to many in our little town.

She tells me of your courtship, a relationship I understand that is built upon computer dates and letters and calls and emails. I asked her once how it was that she fell in love with a man she barely knew since I understood she only met you when Frank drove her back to Texas and she attended your boot camp graduation. I intended no malice with my query and although she chooses to tease me about my reasons for such a question, I think at the time she perceived it as innocent. She smiled with the question and explained that the relationship she had with you was the most honest one she had ever had. She claims there is no pretending between the two of you because of all of the difficult circumstances you both have faced. She said you helped talk her through the anxiety and worry she suffered during her pregnancy. She said you were kind and easy to talk to and that she felt you were sincere in your affections and concern.

She seems to think that because you met each other when you were both heading into new territories, journeying across unknown paths, that there is a bond connecting you and a permission to be completely yourselves. She was pregnant and a new resident in this fair village and you were fighting a war in a strange land. Although she understands the differences in what you have both faced, she said the unfamiliarity of the circumstances and the sense of suddenly being pushed into the world alone somehow connected you in a way that will last forever. I don't claim to know much about romantic relationships but I do know that Trina is loyal and honest and a good judge of character. If she says your hearts are bound together for a lifetime, I believe it.

Your grandmother from Ramah comes to church quite often even though I know the trip is a long one for her, especially in the winter months when I know the roads are icy and difficult to traverse. And yet, she is faithful to the service of Holy Family and to the ways of the Catholic Church. She knows of our prayers for her grandson and enjoys the stories the parishioners love to tell about you while they reminisce of your boyhood times. I guess she didn't see you all that often when you were growing up and these childhood memories seem to bring her great pleasure.

I try to minister to your father, Frank. He is a kind man and has been generous to me in the sharing of his knowledge and skills in working on the engine of my car as he never charges me for auto repairs. He has shared stories and information about your people, the Navajo, and has offered to take me out to wilderness sites that are sacred to your family and that he is sure I would find beautiful. Although I haven't actually gone on any camping adventures with him yet, I look forward to opportunities to see the Malpais area and Fence Lake and the North Plains. I've heard that Frank Twinhorse is the best person to hike and track this county and I am happy that we will have that opportunity in these upcoming spring and summer months. Perhaps you will be home and well soon and can join us in these outings.

Please receive this letter and these included gifts from the church and me as signs of our love and prayers. Please also know that I am extending to you the gift of my friendship as your pastor and as a personal friend of Trina. I know it will take some time to get used to me and my ways as a priest, but I hope you will allow me the chance to minister to you when you return to New Mexico. I have heard so many lovely things about you, your commitment to hard work, your gentle ways with animals, your volunteer work in the community, and your service to the church and I look forward to the opportunity of getting to know you better.

Your choice to serve in the military is an honorable one and I thank you for your willingness to enlist and join the army while we have been at war. I hope you know your efforts, your choice, and your service is honored here at home and across the country. We pray for your healing and for your speedy return to Pie Town.

In God's grace,
Father George Morris, Holy Family Church

Dear Beloved Raymond,

Roger and I are sitting at the kitchen table, late on a Thursday evening, sharing our concerns and love for you as we write this letter together. Roger has asked that I do all the writing because he has such poor penmanship. And if you remember all the notes he scribbled to you across the years, you will surely agree. He's a great man, a wonderful sheriff; but he cannot write a lick. I often wonder how his deputies and secretary ever follow any of his written orders because you can't tell whether he's writing in Spanish or English and it wouldn't matter anyway because I can read both languages, have lived with him for more than thirty years, and I still can't decipher his words. (He just mumbled something in Spanish but it's not worth translating it and adding it to this letter.)

First, just let me say that we love you and we are praying for you. I have placed your name on the prayer lists of every church in Catron County and even some in other places across the state. I also called Angel and told her about your injuries and she has promised to place your name in the prayer box at the church where she goes for weekly meetings. We ask God to heal all of your broken bones and wounds from the accident, to mend you back together and bring you home to us very soon.

Frank told me the details of your injuries and even though I haven't worked as a trauma nurse, I do remember enough from my training to know it will be a long period of rehabilitation and recovery. I say this not as a means to depress you, as Roger is pointing out, but to let you know that if I can do anything to assist the therapists or doctors when you get back to Pie Town, I happily offer all of my services. I have many unused vacation and sick days and I'm sure that my supervisor from the nursing home would allow me to take a leave of absence if you need a private nurse. I will ask Frank to keep me posted on your recovery and if my care is needed, I will make myself available.

Roger says he is happy to drive you around when you get home as long as you don't mind riding in the squad car. He remembers how much you used to enjoy sitting in the back seat, sirens blaring and lights flashing, and he'd be happy to oblige you those pleasures again. I just told him that you were a boy when you rode with him around the county and that I don't think you'd be too keen on all that show and noise since you are now an adult. But now that I write that, I realize that the sirens and lights are still part of the reason Roger enjoys his job; so maybe that's something boys just don't grow out of!

Although she hasn't come right out and asked us, both Roger and I get the feeling that since you may be coming home soon, Trina is thinking about moving from the garage apartment into Roger's house. We're not sure of what she is expecting regarding your living arrangements but we do know she would want you to be able to visit her. We are, of course, happy to make that possible. In the house, everything is all on one level, after all, and would be easily accessible if you are in a wheelchair and need those capabilities. Roger and I have talked about it and even without a wheelchair, we can't see how you could maneuver those stairs to the apartment. If this is what she wants, we will support her in this move. It's easy to see that she cares a great deal for you and we're happy that the two of you found each other and have supported each other through war and birth. It took longer than it should have but Roger and I realize now how lucky we are to have each other and we both regret what was lost in our time apart. We both agree that there is nothing better than a good partner in life.

We're still working full-time. His sheriff duties keep him very busy and even though he's hired a couple of new deputies it seems he has to take care of something for the department every day. I asked him just now when the last time was that he took an entire day off and he can't remember having one. We are hoping that in the spring and summer we'll both take some vacation and go to Denver to visit Angel and have some nice time with her.

I guess you may be wondering how our daughter is faring in Colorado and we're happy to report that we feel like she's doing better now. After Alex died and she didn't even show up for her own son's funeral, we lost touch with her for almost a year. And then, out of the blue, she called and claimed she was in a good program, clean and sober, working at a coffee house, and living in a nice home with five or six other recovering addicts. We've seen her once or twice since that call. She came home for the holidays this year, just for a couple of days, and we met her in Santa Fe a few months ago when she caught a ride with a friend who was driving down. She's still rail thin, but she doesn't look so haggard any longer and even if I am her mother, I still say she's beautiful like her grandmother and as smart as her father. All I really think that she inherited from me is her feisty temper and her way with horses. Roger just said, amen to that, by the way.

Of course, we both know it was you who taught her everything she knows about riding. I tried to show her all my tricks and ideas about horses but by the time she was six she had her own way of doing things and her own way of doing things did not include her mother. Roger and I often talk about how grateful we are to you and Frank, the way you took care of our Angel, the friendship the two of you shared as children. You really are more like brother and sister than me and Lawrence ever were and I know she misses you and I know she would want me to send her love.

Roger and I were just talking about the fact that she didn't take much with her when she left after Alex was born. She didn't want the furniture we bought her or any of the clothes she had made or bought with her own money. She left the gold crucifix necklace her grandfather gave her when she turned sixteen and the set of pearl earrings Roger and I bought for her when she gave birth to Alex. The jewelry her grandmother gave her, the rings and pins her boyfriends had bought her over the years, she left them all in the little jewelry box on her dresser. But the one thing I know she still has, the one thing she has never lost, left behind, given away, or put aside is that leather bracelet you made her when the two of you turned sixteen. I remember how much it meant to her when you gave it to her, how she explained to us where you found the silver charm, a bear, you bought from a silversmith at the Gathering of the Nations Pow-Wow in Albuquerque and the tiny piece of turquoise you found on one of your trips out in the Narrows, the one you polished and placed just beside the charm. As far as I know, she still wears it, the leather worn and the piece of turquoise, thin from so many years of wear and tear. Still, I like the thought that this is the piece of jewelry she keeps. I have found great comfort, especially in the years when we didn't know where she was, didn't know how she was, that she was wearing the bracelet that you made for her, a bracelet that promised protection from all harm. You are the best friend Angel has ever had. Your father was the best godfather a child could ever know; and I have always thanked God for having the two of you in our lives and in the life of our daughter.

I don't know why I'm rambling on and on about Angel when this letter is supposed to be a letter of encouragement and well-wishes, a letter to let you know about how we're doing. I guess I just got sidetracked and took a little trip down memory lane. You would think that Roger would have headed me off and pointed me in the right direction but I guess we both love you for many reasons and a lot of them have to do with what you did for our daughter.

We will be here for you when you get home. We will do whatever you need for us to do, to take care of you, to provide you with housing, transportation, home health-care, and even a babysitter for Alexandria so that you and Trina can have some quality time to spend together. You are like a son to us, Raymond Twinhorse. It will always be that way.

Be well. Come home soon. Know of our love. Roger just gave me a nod that the letter is fine. So, I will say our good-byes.

  Love,

  Roger and Malene

Ah-hah-lah'nih!
Greetings my son,

Trina is putting together a nice bundle of letters and gifts from the people in Pie Town. I feel a bit odd contributing to this community endeavor but Trina has insisted I participate and include a letter with everyone else. I try to explain to her that you and I have never written letters but she will not let me out of this opportunity to send a father's own personal wishes for his son's well-being.

The garage still provides me with a good working wage and I remain able to slide under the chassis and also lift off all four wheels for rotation; so I guess I will continue with my employment for a while longer. Trina is a solid employee, has good work habits, and has learned practically everything I know about engines in her short time at the garage. I suspect she will know more than I once she starts working on the newer models and learns the ins and outs of computer-generated systems. She has small hands which I now see is a favorable attribute for reaching beneath hoses and behind radiators, and in between spark plugs. She is strong as well and can lean over hoods and motors far longer than I. It is not a natural thing for me to be around a woman for so much of the day, but I find her company pleasant and the sharing of the workload a relief.

I talk to your doctor or a nurse there at the hospital every couple of days or so. I am not sure that you remember the conversation you and I had when you were first transferred to Germany, as you seemed a bit groggy from the medication and the trip from Afghanistan, but I cannot say how much it meant to hear your voice. Even with the reports of your recovery, the high marks of surgical success you have had, and the cheerful voices of your caregivers, I have been anxious until I finally heard you speak. It was a great comfort to me.

I have been to Ramah. I know that my refusal to visit our family has been a source of discontent for you for a very long time. I know we have not seen eye to eye about my choices to leave the reservation and to live away from your grandparents and our extended family members. I need to say that I have been wrong about that matter and I have sought to reconcile with your grandmother, my mother, and I will seek to make things right for you and the others as well. I see how important it is to have that support, especially now, especially as you are so far away, and we cannot get to you. Your grandmother sends her deepest love and has asked that you come back to Ramah and live with them when you return.

Even though I do not know if you have decided where you will live when you return, I have not mentioned your relationship with Trina to her. I feel that is not my news to report and I will let you see your own way to discuss this with her. I am, of course, hoping you will return to live with me in the trailer, the way it was before you left for the army and I am already making necessary arrangements for you to be able to transfer a wheelchair easily inside, in case you are still in need of one when you come home. Bernie King is helping me widen the front door and build a ramp but I am still unsure of how we can maneuver the chair through the narrow hallway. Perhaps, it is time, as Trina likes to tell me, to buy a real house that cannot be toppled in the spring winds or hooked up to a truck and pulled away. I try to explain my love for the brown trailer, but she says she spent too many years of her childhood parked in a trailer court and will never make her home in another one as long as she lives. I guess that's information you might need to know in case your relationship continues to grow. You will not bring her as your bride into a mobile home.

Ah, but what do I know about brides and such? Your mother never mentioned any discontent she may have had in living in a trailer so far away from everyone. She told me when we first moved in that she liked the privacy of our lives, the way she could see and count the stars, the sound of desert wind, the long setting of the sun, the sheer hold that silence can have on a person. I never understood, of course, why she left when she did. I never knew she was unhappy or displeased with our life and

as I have told you more than once, it never had anything
to do with you. I claim all responsibility for her departure and I hope you never entertained a single thought
that it had anything to do with you. She loved you from
the moment she knew she was pregnant. I just think the
weight of being married to me, the deep longing she had
for her family and the inability to find her place in Catron
County just became more than she could bear. I no
longer even blame my relatives for pushing her away. "It
is the curious nature of many unknown things to remain
unknown," as your great grandfather used to say.

If I knew where to reach her, of course, I would let her
know of your military service and of the recent events in
your life. Even though I never told you this news, I tried
to find her when you graduated from high school, having
made your plans for joining the army, but I was unable to
locate her then and I must admit I haven't really tried in
many months. However, if that is something you would
like for me to do before you return home, I will happily
search for her again.

I know she would be proud of you, as proud as I am.
She would think you are brave and selfless to do what you
have done. She would surely hold your face in her hands
and smile that beautiful smile at you, whispering those
things she told you when you were a baby that she never
repeated to me. I hope you know she always loved you.

I have been tracking the coyotes for the past few
months since I still struggle with sleeplessness. As you
discovered when you were a boy, on those dark nights
when I can no longer stay put in my bed, I wander the

early morning hours along the hidden trails. The animals have become used to me now and do not even seem to mind when I join them on their hunts. I do believe that the leader of this small group is from the same pack that we met on a trail a few years ago, just before the spring of your departure. Do you remember the family? And do you recall the smallest pup, the one who lagged the farthest behind the others, the one we left our sandwiches for? There was a small ring of white fur around his silver-brown neck. I do believe he is full-grown now and leads this pack I follow. It is odd to say, of course, but it is as if he recognizes me. And all these seasons later, I feel connected to this animal as if we shared something we both can never forget. I even find myself telling him of you as I sense his questioning of why I walk alone. Where it was that we once shared our pity with him because of his small size, his inability to run as quickly as the other coyotes, I feel his pity for me now that I travel with no pack. I suppose that is why I am allowed to track and hunt with him.

I have also seen the old witch running along the canyon floor and the wisp of smoke that you always called "Kit Carson's ghost" that seems to waft along the north end of the ranch at the Old Sheep Trail. I still find the mounds of rocks that you made as a boy to mark paths for you and Angel to find your way home when you wandered for so many miles. I see all the places we shared, all the trails we walked, the clearings where we rested for the night; and when I lie beneath the stars, so many of them, you know, I call up your name to our ancestors, to the spirits to guide you and protect you and bring you out of harm's way and back home. I cannot say if I think there is one God watching the world as the white man seems so resolved to make everyone acknowledge and believe in; but I confess to you, I have even prayed to Him.

You are my family, Raymond. You are my son. And I yearn to have you home.

Ah-hah-lah'nih! I will greet you with love and great favor when we meet again.

Your father, Frank Twinhorse

Dear Raymond,

I have no idea if this box of letters and stuff makes it to you. The address the hospital nurse repeated for me has so many numbers and letters and has that German name for a town, I don't know if I got everything right on the label or not. Christine helped me. She read what I had written over and over to me while I wrote the address on the right forms and then checked the label side by side with my notes from the phone call and she promises me I got it right, so I hope that is true.

In case you're wondering, I did write the label and got the box before I wrote my own letter. I sometimes have a hard time writing down a lot in one sitting but I guess you've figured that out since I tend to do most of my catching you up on the town and my life when we talk on the computer. I know that you said the last time we had a conversation that I should write longer letters but it's just hard for me to get it all down in words. And plus, you know how challenging spelling can be for me! Malene let me have the old computer that Alex had and she showed me the tool bar where you can check your spelling, but as you can see, I'll still not likely get all the words written correct. Maybe you're banged up enough not to notice. Not that I hope that, of course. See, I'm such an idiot. Who would say something as stupid as that? At least, when I'm talking I can take it back. When I'm writing, it's too hard to erase a whole sentence. Anyway, maybe I should learn to use the computer better if I have to write you a lot of letters. Christine told me you can take away entire lines and paragraphs if you read it later and want to change things. She forgot to show me that tool bar, however, before she left for her shift at the nursing home. So, just forgive my dumb mistakes. I'm real good at running that numbers program for the garage but when it comes to typing up a letter using that long typing software, that's another whole story.

Oris said he was writing a letter. Francine is doing one and Father George, Roger and Malene and Frank are contributing. I have no idea what kinds of stuff they'll be telling you about me and Alexandria. And I may read Oris' before I mail it. He sometimes says more than he ought to say. I know that some of them are sending you a few things too since I told them that I was mailing everything in a box and they can include gifts if they wanted. Francine wants to send a pie and I'll do my best to get it wrapped good, but if it's gotten turned over or squashed in between all the other stuff, just get one of the nurses to throw it away and tell Francine you can't eat pie because of your hospital diet.

Are you on a hospital diet? What do they feed you in Germany? Is it the same food as you get in the army dining room or is it better? Oh, I don't know why I'm writing you questions. I guess it's just my mind thinking of things, thinking of you and what you're doing all day now that you're wounded.

Alexandria drew you a picture. It's mostly just red and blue lines of coloring but she seemed real intent on making you a pretty picture so just think of it as a special portrait from your favorite girl. I hung your army photograph on the refrigerator door and every time I get her juice or some milk, I show her your face and say your name. One day a week or so ago, I swear she said "Waymon," and that should make you feel pretty good because she hasn't yet said anybody else's name. Francine keeps trying to get her to call out "Aunt Francie" but even though Alexandria makes a lot of noise and you'd think she's really talking, she doesn't know many words and "Fr's" are a little hard for her, I think.

She recognizes faces, of course. That's the easy part for her. And she gets picked up and toted by just about everybody in Pie Town; so the good thing is that she's not afraid of anybody. I guess that's a good thing. 'Course, I'll have to keep a close eye on her if we ever go to a big city or something. She could easily crawl into the arms of the wrong person with that trusting nature of hers.

Frank and I still work together and we're still eating our lunch together every day. We don't say a lot about you and the accident. I think talking about it makes him nervous. And when he's nervous, he just walks out of the garage, heading north. I never know if he's coming back and I should wait on him or if I should just finish what I'm doing, close the garage, and go home. I told him one time just to let me know when he was leaving but it's like he just all of a sudden gets a queer thought in his head and has to get out in the hills. I had an uncle like that too but he'd been locked up for a long time. I think he just needed to make good use of his freedom. I don't know about Frank. I guess he just finds more comfort being with the animals, away from the people, than he does sharing his company with the folks from town. I do know he worries about you even though he never lets on as such.

I'm real glad he approves of the two of us together. I don't usually care what most people think of me; but I care what Frank thinks. Him and Roger, Malene, Francine, Christine, Fred and Bea, I feel like I have a family here. I feel like I'm a part of something I've never had and I guess that means I care how they think I'm doing.

They all love you, that's for sure. I mean, I knew it when you left for boot camp. I heard all the stuff they said about you joining the army and everything but since they all heard about you getting hurt, everybody has to stop and tell me and Frank how much you mean to them and how they're all praying for you. It's a nice thing, Raymond. I hope you know what you mean to the folks here.

Father George asked me the other day how I fell in love with you. I told him about our talks and how nice you've always been to me, how it never seemed to bother you that I was pregnant. But he seemed so curious about how we could be as close as we are when we haven't really spent that much time together. I told him that I thought we had a lot in common, that we seemed to see the world kind of alike. I also told him that I wasn't trying so hard to impress you, to be something I'm not and that you seemed just fine with that. I told him that can make a girl fall in love more than anything. And then I asked him why he wanted to know so much and whether he was thinking about leaving the priesthood and hooking up with Bea's niece from Socorro who has started coming to church quite a bit. He blushed when I asked him the question and it was the funniest thing. We were eating dinner together at the diner and he ran out of there so fast he forgot to pay his bill. I tell him that he still owes me for that dinner. And I get a big kick out of that for sure.

I called a travel agent last week in Albuquerque to find out how much it would cost for me to come to Germany. It was a whole lot of money. I know I could ask everybody to chip in and help me buy the ticket but I don't know if you even want me to visit you. I know that when I feel bad I'm not really interested in entertaining company, not that you'd have to entertain me, but still, you know what I mean. So, I'm just going to wait and let you tell me if you want me to come or not. I got a Visa card when I went to work with Frank; so I can just charge the ticket if you want me to come. Just let me know.

I can't stand not hearing from you every day like I

used to. I hate not knowing what you're thinking, how bad you're hurting and what you feel like. I guess I've gotten accustomed to having you a part of my every day; and even when we're not talking, I still think of myself as coming home to you, that you're waiting for me, waiting to tell me something about those crazy guys you run with and the way it is over there. I still have all these stories I want to tell you about Alexandria, about the new thing I learned about a V–8 engine or a European-made motor, the crazy joke Oris told. You've become such a part of my life, Raymond, I can't imagine not having you in it. So, you get better, you hear me? You get better and come home. Me and Alexandria need you.

Okay, that's enough. I'm going to try and get Christine to take a good picture of me this evening before I mail the box. So that means I've got to go take a shower, wash my hair, and put on something decent. I don't want you to hang some photograph of me wearing my coveralls and looking like a boy. Then what would your buddies think?

I love you, Raymond. Please come home soon.

Trina

Read on for a sneak peek at
Lynne Hinton's upcoming novel,
WELCOME BACK TO PIE TOWN
On sale July 2012
From William Morrow Paperbacks

Chapter Four

FATHER GEORGE MORRIS was reading scripture when the power went out. The tea kettle was whistling, and he had put his Bible down and was preparing to get up from his desk and walk into the kitchen to have a cup of tea.

"Ah, Lord, the storms of summertime." He sighed. He reached into one of the desk drawers, found a flashlight, turned it on, and made his way into the kitchen. After pouring himself a cup of tea, he began feeling his way through the cabinets for the candles he knew were kept above the stove.

He found a few votive candles and placed them on small plates, lighting them with the matches he had collected from his desk drawer. He set the candles around the front room of the rectory and sat back down at his desk, the cup of tea beside his Bible. He thought about the scripture he was reading, the Gospel of Mark, and particularly the story of Jesus walking on the water, the

story of high winds and fear, a storm experienced by the
disciples. He thought of the irony of his reading about a
storm, considering what was happening all around him,
and had to smile. He opened his Bible to read more but
then, realizing that he would not be able to read with so
little light, closed the book and considered just going to
bed, even though he wasn't actually sleepy.

He thought of the events of the day, the meeting of
the education committee and the decision to start a
nursery for the worship hour on Sunday mornings. He
thought about his visit to the parish in Quemado and
his conversation with Father Quy, the priest serving the
two other churches in the vicinity. He recalled the man's
cynical comment that Father George had a cushy job
serving only the Holy Family Church in Pie Town, not
being responsible to the diocese in Gallup, and how it
seemed that Father George had taken to radical ways by
not wearing his collar and allowing Protestants to share
in regular worship.

George had chosen not to engage with the other priest
once he made those remarks. He knew that the other
parish priests in New Mexico and the entire Southwest
thought the arrangement in Pie Town with the diocese in
Gallup was inappropriate and out of line. He knew that
Holy Family Church was a kind of renegade organization
that even seemed close to breaking ties with the Catholic
Church. He understood that once he and the citizens of
Pie Town chose to build their own church, without super-
vision or assistance from the diocese in Gallup, he and
the Church were moving into uncharted territory. Father

George still referred to himself as a Catholic priest, but he was not in full standing with the Church. It was a unique and precarious relationship, and many other priests were not happy about it.

George had tried to build a friendship with the new priest in Catron County when he arrived, but the orthodox young man, trained in his home country of Vietnam, could never understand the role of the priest in Pie Town. George had decided after this last visit that he would make no further attempts at being friends. He was, after all, deeply involved in the lives of his parishioners, in the events of the community, and happily, he noted to himself, had more than enough friends. If Father Quy wanted to make a connection with George, he knew how to contact him. Pie Town wasn't that far from Quemado.

George looked at his watch, trying to make out the time, and took a sip of tea. He thought about his afternoon, his visit to Frank Twinhorse's garage. He had taken in the station wagon he had been driving for the entire time he had been in Catron County. It had not been a reliable vehicle when it was given to him by the Monsignor in Gallup, and now it was simply falling apart.

That afternoon, George had taken his car in because the brakes were squealing. Since he didn't know a drum from a pedal, and since he needed his car the rest of the week, he was hoping that Trina or Frank would be able to tighten something or oil a part and take care of the problem quickly. He was hopeful that he wouldn't have to leave it with them for any length of time.

Trina, the young woman who had arrived in Pie Town

at the same time that Father George had, was working at the garage. She was good at what she did, loved working on engines, and had learned a lot about auto mechanics while serving an apprenticeship with Frank. She had, in fact, replaced more parts in the station wagon than George could count and had practically rebuilt the transmission earlier in the year. She was quite skilled at her work and very happy in her new job.

When he arrived at the garage, Trina and Frank were nowhere to be found. He called out for them, walked around the bays and into the office, but neither of them answered or showed up. Finally, just as he was getting into the station wagon to leave, Frank pulled up in his tow truck, explaining briefly that Trina was home with Raymond and that she had called Frank over to handle a situation.

Father George knew that Raymond, Frank's son and Trina's boyfriend, had been in Pie Town for only about five weeks. The church had thrown a big "welcome home" party for the wounded soldier when he was released from the Veterans Hospital in Albuquerque, and even though the young man seemed a bit uncomfortable with the attention from his hometown, he acted like he enjoyed the gathering. He was quiet but did not seem troubled, shy but not necessarily withdrawn.

George had visited Raymond while he was hospitalized and had seen the physical wounds of war. The young soldier had been in a vehicle that exploded because of a roadside bomb. He was the only one who had survived. His left knee was shattered. Both lungs were punctured.

There was significant hearing loss, a fractured skull, brain trauma, and more than eight or nine other broken bones. Raymond had come through numerous surgeries and had been sent home after lengthy stays at medical clinics and hospitals in Afghanistan, Germany, North Carolina, and finally Albuquerque.

Father George had concluded, even though there had been no real cause for his suspicions, that Raymond had suffered as much, if not more, emotionally as physically during his short time of service in war, and after his visit in Albuquerque he had suggested to Trina and Frank that the young man might benefit from support services offered to returning veterans. Both the boy's father and his girlfriend had explained that they mentioned this to Raymond, but that he seemed unwilling to consider talking about his experience with anyone.

Once Raymond had been home a few weeks, he became increasingly withdrawn, and Father George started paying closer attention. He checked on the young man every couple of days, and even though Raymond wouldn't look George in the eye and seemed unable to sit still for any length of time, the priest thought everything was going as well as could be expected. He had not seen signs of real trauma for the soldier.

"What kind of situation?" George remembered asking Frank.

The father wouldn't answer any questions about his son. He had checked the station wagon and announced that the priest would need new brake liners on the rear wheels. He could leave the car at the garage until the parts arrived and were installed, he was informed, or it was probably safe to drive around town if he wanted to return later in the week. George had decided just to keep the car until the parts were delivered.

"Would it help if I visited?" he had asked Frank before driving off. He knew where Trina and Raymond lived. He knew they had moved out of the little garage apartment and into Roger's house, since the sheriff had moved in with Malene once they got married. "I can drop by, offer to talk to Raymond, offer to drive him to Albuquerque to talk to someone there."

And George, sipping some more of his tea, recalled how Frank appeared when the offer was made. He had looked away and then turned back, shaking his head from side to side. He had taken a long breath before answering, wiping his hands on the rag hanging from his pocket.

"I like you, Father George. I have since you built the church and did what you did for this little town. I respect your work." He stepped away from the car. "You have a good heart."

George glanced away.

And then Frank had hesitated before finishing. He shook his head again. "But you can't help my son." He then slid his hand across the back of his neck. "I'm not sure what or who can help him now." And with that, Frank had turned away and walked into the office. George had waited, thinking he might return, but when he didn't, George had simply driven off.

Father George considered that perhaps he should have

gone over to Trina's. He didn't need a reason to visit; the young couple knew the priest often stopped by to see parishioners or community members. They both knew he sometimes dropped in on folks without calling ahead. But George had chosen not to meddle, not that time. He told himself he would wait until he gained permission from Trina or Raymond to step in and offer help.

He had decided that the most he could do at the time, the best he had to offer, was to simply say his prayers. And so, there in the meek light of small candles, that's what he did. Father George dropped his face, closed his eyes, and folded his hands. Cloaked in darkness, he prayed.

Home Sweet Home

CANDIS TERRY

This is dedicated to the men, women, and families of the Idaho Army National Guard at Gowen Field and the Mountain Home Air Force Base. Please accept my heartfelt thanks for your service and dedication. You keep us safe. You make us proud. God bless.

Chapter One

W**HEN YOU GREW** up in a town the size of a flea circus anonymity was impossible.

There hadn't been a chance in hell he could have slipped back in unnoticed. As an Army Ranger, Lieutenant Aiden Marshall had been to some of the most hellish corners on earth and no one had been the wiser. Except for maybe the enemy. Yet the moment he'd cranked the key in the ignition of his old pickup, it seemed the entire population of Sweet, Texas, had heard the engine catch.

Today he'd traded his fatigues for an old T-shirt and Levi's, but the dog tags pressed against his heart verified he'd be a soldier until the day they put him in the earth.

He was damned lucky he wasn't already there.

As he drove the winding road through pastures where longhorns grazed, he did not take for granted the faded yellow ribbons hugging the trunks of the large oaks that bordered the road. Those ribbons had been placed there for him and two of his best buddies. They'd all enlisted the same day. Survived boot camp and Ranger training together. Hit the sands of Afghanistan as one. Fought side-by-side.

He'd been the only one to make it home.

In the trenches they'd added one more friend to their unit. One more who'd proven faithful and trustworthy. One who'd offered comfort on dark nights and lonely days.

One more Aiden had to leave behind.

The pressure in his chest tightened as he lifted his hand in a wave to the group of seniors in jogging shoes waiting to cross the road. On the way to his destination, he could not ignore the joy on the faces of those who waved or shouted "welcome back" as he passed by. Those in his community knew none of the anguish that kept him awake night after night. They were just happy he had made it home.

His hometown had been hit hard by the loss of two upstanding soldiers, men who'd been his brothers-in-arms. Men he'd been honored to serve with. As a survivor, he felt none of the joy and all of the guilt. The hardest thing he'd had to face upon his return was the visits he'd paid to those heroes' families. Looking them in the eye and expressing his sorrow for their loss when so much of it had been caused by his own miscalculations. Yet they'd taken him into their arms, offering *him* consolation he did not deserve. The thought still took his breath away.

On Main Street, beneath the old water tower where local businesses displayed patriotic signs and the flagpole in Town Square flew a pristine Stars and Stripes, Aiden eased his truck into the gravel lot beside Bud's Nothing Finer Diner. Over the years the good people of Sweet had tried their best to make the town appeal to tourists. The apple orchards—like the one his family owned—had blossomed into bed-and-breakfasts, art galleries, antique shops, and wine rooms. Judging by the near-empty streets, the place still had a long way to go.

In a space near the door he cut the truck's engine, leaned back in the seat, and inhaled the aroma of chicken-fried steak that floated in through the window on the warm summer breeze. Bud's Diner was little more than a yellow concrete box, but since the day Aiden had been old enough to sit at the counter, he'd enjoyed extra thick milkshakes and homemade eats that made his mouth water. Even when he'd been halfway across the world. Bud's was the first place the townsfolk gathered to mourn, celebrate, or discuss local politics.

He snatched the keys from the ignition and opened the door. Through six tours and countless missions in the Middle East, his mouth had watered for a slice of home. He was about to get his wish.

The bell above the door announced his arrival to the farmers and community members who huddled inside around tables nicked and scarred by years of diners with eager appetites. Marv Woodrow, a World War II vet, stood on feeble legs and gave him a salute. Bill McBride, a Vietnam vet, stood and gave him a one-armed hug and a fist bump. The rest also welcomed him home as he made his way to the counter. He graciously accepted their warm reception, though the soldier and friend inside of him rebelled.

Why was he still here when his friends were not?

He glanced around the diner at the wood-paneled walls and the Don't-Mess-with-Texas decor. As wonderful as the greetings had been, there was one welcome he'd looked forward to the most. Even though he wouldn't enjoy giving her the news he had to share.

Back in the kitchen a good-natured argument surfaced.

"Pick up your own danged pickles, Bud. I've got my hands full of Arlene's sweet potato fries, a buffalo burger, and Walter's patty melt."

"But the pickles are burnin' in the fryer, girl."

A feminine sigh of exasperation lifted above the lunchtime chatter and forks clanging on plates. At the sound, the tightness in Aiden's chest eased, and a rare smile pushed at the corners of his mouth. Before he could breathe, the owner of that sassy tone marched out of the kitchen.

"Here's your melt, Walter." She set an overflowing plate down in front of the old guy at the end of the counter. "Don't be surprised if that hunk of meat finds its way back to the cow before Bud gets movin' back there."

Aiden picked up the plastic-coated menu he could recite blindfolded and watched her work. Quick hands. Sweet smile. Thick honey-colored hair pulled up into a ponytail that swung across her back. A pair of jeans hugged her slender thighs. A yellow *Bud's Diner* T-shirt molded to her full breasts and small waist.

Good thing he was sitting down because his lower half was definitely standing at attention.

She swiped a towel over a newly vacated seat near the end of the counter. Catching a glimpse of a new customer from the corner of her eye, she drawled, "I'll be right with ya, darlin'."

Two seconds later she set down the towel, pulled her order pad from the pocket of her apron, and made her way toward his end of the counter.

"What can I . . ." Pencil poised, her blue eyes lifted and that beautiful, plump mouth slid into a warm smile. "You're back," she said in a slow whisper.

A quick heartbeat passed while her gaze ate him up.

Then, before he could blink, she launched herself into his arms.

FROM THE MOMENT she'd figured out the difference between boys and girls, Paige Walker had known what she wanted in life.

And what she wanted was Aiden Marshall.

He'd been a rough-and-tumble boy who'd escaped her amorous intentions in elementary school when she'd tried to talk him into kissing her behind the cafeteria. She'd finally caught him in high school, where *he* became the teacher and *she* the willing student in their kissing lessons. They'd been together almost every day until the darkest day in America crashed down in the nightmare no one had ever expected. The following week Aiden, Billy Marks, and Bobby Hansen enlisted in the Army.

When Aiden had left for boot camp he made her no promises. Once he'd been approved for Ranger training his infrequent letters dwindled. Over the past couple of years he'd barely sent more than a quick note or two. Though he'd told her not to, she'd promised him that she would wait.

And she had.

As his strong arms curled around her and tucked her in close, she knew all those lonely nights she'd waited with worry and fear burrowed into her heart had been worth every second.

Aiden was home.

Paige pressed her cheek against his faded T-shirt and listened to the steady heartbeat in his chest. She inhaled the fresh scent of his soap and his underlying masculine heat. With a sigh she leaned her head back and looked up at him while her fingers molded around his hard, defined biceps.

A man like Aiden was impossible to ignore, unless you had severely poor eyesight, or you just didn't care for a guy with a movie star face and a body honed for elite military missions. On top of all that he had the most amazing mouth—lips that knew how to give a girl a kiss she'd remember until one day she could kiss him again. Today he'd discarded his army fatigues and settled into a worn pair of Levi's that accented his long, muscular legs and cupped his generous package like a lover's hand. He looked so good she wanted to lay him down on the counter and feast on him like an all-you-can-eat Sunday buffet.

On a good day Aiden's short dark hair and the spark in his brown eyes could stun the breath in her lungs. She hadn't seen him in over two years—when last he'd come home to his dying father's bedside. Since then hell had broken loose. Today while he stood close enough for her to touch and hold, Paige knew in her heart Aiden Marshall was a changed man.

While she told herself it only mattered that he was safe and everything would be just fine, her fears resurfaced.

Aiden may be home.

But the smile in his eyes had vanished.

Chapter Two

AFTER SEVERAL HOURS and several slices of apple crumb pie à la mode, Aiden and his full stomach leaned back in the chair. He listened while Hazel and Ray Calhoun excitedly described how the senior center had contacted a new TV makeover show to try to put a better face on their small town and increase the tourism. Aiden couldn't imagine why Hollywood would ever come this far south. It only mattered that the folks in this town and other small towns across America cared enough to try to make things better. These hard-working, generous-hearted people were the reason he, Billy, and Bobby had enlisted.

A dainty hand with clean, short nails settled over his shoulder. He looked up into the blue eyes he'd dreamed of on many a lonely night. A sudden jolt struck him in the center of his chest. Paige had always had a way of doing that to him. Even now when he knew the heart had been ripped out of him and he had nothing left to give.

"If y'all are done monopolizing the lieutenant's time, I'd like to borrow him for a bit," Paige said in a teasing drawl. "But only if that's all right."

"Oh pooh." Gertie West wrinkled up her nose. "We were just getting to the good stuff."

Aiden glanced out the front window where the sun hung low in the sky. As much as he'd like to, he couldn't put off the conversation he and Paige needed to have any longer. It would be unfair to her and selfish of him.

He stood and pushed the chair back. "I really do need to get going."

"You come back tomorrow, young man," Ray Calhoun said. "We want to hear all about your adventures."

Adventures.

Not exactly what he'd call them.

Wasn't likely he'd discuss them either.

He gave the afternoon diners at the table a nod and turned toward Paige.

"Come with me." She smiled wide enough to flash those pretty white teeth. "I have something I want to show you."

"Your car or mine?"

She slipped her hand into his and tugged him toward the door. "How about for old time's sake we take your truck?"

A sensual flood of memories he thought he'd buried long ago popped up fresh like a spring daisy. "Sun's still shining." He smiled and gave her hand a squeeze. "I think the population of Sweet might take offense to you whipping off that T-shirt."

"Wouldn't be the first time." She grinned. "Now come on. We're wasting daylight."

As she tugged him through the gravel parking lot, he watched the way her hips swayed. Nothing outrageously obvious. Just a smooth motion that belied the passion lit deep in her core. He'd almost forgotten all the little idiosyncrasies she possessed. Like the way she lifted her arms toward the moon when she was on top of him, giving him the best sex of his life. Or the way she'd snuggle right against his side and drape her smooth leg over his hips. Or even the way she'd reach for him in her sleep, then sigh when she found him.

He'd carried those memories with him through boot camp. Through extensive Ranger training. Through numerous deployments to Iraq and Afghanistan. Then one day everything around him exploded. After that, he hadn't allowed himself to think of the things that had made him happy. He didn't deserve to be happy. Not when those closest to him—those he was supposed to protect—were no longer able to have happy thoughts.

Without hesitation, Paige climbed up into his truck and slid right to the middle where she'd always sat. When he moved onto the seat beside her, she grinned like someone had just handed her a present. His hand paused on the key in the ignition.

How the hell could he even consider breaking her heart?

He didn't want to.

But it had to be done.

Chapter Three

PAIGE TRIED TO remain positive, though Aiden's smile had once again disappeared. She knew the hell he'd been through from the stories his brother Ben had relayed. She knew she couldn't expect him to just come home and they'd pick up where they'd left off. From the moment she'd heard the news that his duties had been served and he intended to leave the military, she'd made a vow that no matter what, she'd keep a smile on her face. For both of them. She'd see him through whatever demons he had to face. Because there had never been a doubt that she loved him with her whole heart. And nothing could ever take that away.

She leaned forward and turned up the radio while Keith Urban sang about days going by. "Hang a right on Dandelion Street."

Aiden turned his head and looked at her with those deep brown eyes that made her think of the many wonderful nights she'd spent with him looking down at her while their bodies spoke the oldest language in the universe. "You moved?"

She nodded as the truck rambled down her street. "A little over a year ago."

"You still have Cricket?" he asked of the border collie mix she'd rescued from the shelter.

"Of course. She's still got a good amount of crazy going on, but age seems to have settled her down a bit."

"Happens to the best of us, I guess."

"Pull in there." She pointed toward the long gravel driveway that invited visitors up to the gingerbread Victorian that sat behind a white picket fence.

Aiden ducked his head to get a better look through the windshield. "Isn't this your Aunt Bertie's place?"

"Was." Paige reached down and grabbed her purse from the floorboard. "Aunt Bertie developed dementia and we had to put her in assisted care. She needed the money so I bought the place. Come on. I'll show you around."

"You bought this?" He got out of the truck and looked up at the two-story house. "On a waitress's salary?"

"Shocking isn't it?" While he stood there gawking, she walked around the front of the truck, took his hand, and led him toward the front door. "Actually, I bought it on the salary I make at Bud's, plus the money I make doing taxes and accounting for a few local businesses. I make money from the apple orchard too."

"Taxes?"

"Oooh." She laughed at the sudden wrinkle between his eyes. "You look so surprised. I like that."

"I do remember you skipped out on geometry class more than once and that you never liked math."

"That was before I realized the benefits." She turned the key in the lock and pushed the door open. "I completed my bachelor's via the Internet," she explained. "I'm now the proud owner of a business administration degree. Got a gold tassel and everything."

He stepped inside the foyer, gave a slow whistle, and rocked back on the heels of his worn cowboy boots. "You're a very impressive woman, Paige Walker."

"I know." The praise made her smile. "But you'd better be careful because I have a whole bunch of *impressive* up my sleeve just waiting to be unleashed."

He didn't need to ask what she meant. He'd seen her *impressive* side before. She only hoped he'd want to see it again.

A glimmer lit up his eyes and hope warmed in her heart. She reached out, took his hand, and gave him the nickel tour of Honey Hill—named after the honeycrisp apples that grew in the orchard back between the barn and the creek. The place was way more than she needed right now. But she had big plans. Always the optimist, she'd purchased the oversized home. With *him* in mind.

LATER, ON THE back veranda, Aiden lifted the chilled bottle of Sam Adams to his lips and drank. The beer tasted crisp and smooth. The phenomenal view of Paige's backyard offered a lush landscape accented by rows and rows of apple trees laden with ripening fruit. Curled up at his feet lay Cricket, Paige's brown-and-black-spotted border collie. While Paige had gone inside to throw together a meal for them to share, he and Cricket played fetch with a slobbered-up tennis ball. A heaving sigh lifted the dog's broad chest. Apparently he'd worn her out, as now her breathing was deep and even. Not a single brown eyebrow or white paw twitched or moved.

On impulse he reached down and combed his fingers through her soft fur. When she looked up at him with those deep brown eyes, a fist grabbed hold of his heart and squeezed. He'd always thought of himself as a man who could handle anything. But lately his losses refused to lessen their grip on his conscience.

"Need a refill?" Paige asked as she came toward the wrought-iron patio set where he sat. Her hands balanced plates of plump, juicy pieces of barbecued chicken and a mountainous glob of potato salad.

He lifted the bottle. "I'm good."

She set the plates down, and the aroma wafted up and tickled his appetite. "I don't suppose there were many beers to be found in the Middle East."

"Not really. Lots of sand to chew on, though."

She flashed a quick smile as she sat down opposite him and handed him a fork and knife. Earlier at Bud's he'd had a large helping of chicken-fried steak and several pieces of pie. Yet as the sweet honey flavor of the barbecue rolled across his tongue, he felt like a starving man.

"Good thing I cooked last night." She sipped from her wine glass. "Or this would be carrot sticks and Goldfish crackers."

"Didn't you used to eat those all the time in high school?"

"Yep. They even make them in rainbow colors now." She grinned. "You can have a different color for every meal."

He laughed. "Only *you* could make a feast out of a baked cracker."

"I can make a meal out of chocolate chip cookies too. Speaking of, did you get the packages I sent?"

"Yes. Thank you. I shared. Your oatmeal raisin cookies and the teriyaki jerky went over the best with the boys." She took a bite of chicken then looked up with a glimmer of mischief in her blue eyes. "Good thing I checked the guidelines before I sent those girly magazines."

"Yeah, totally against the rules." He chuckled. "But definitely would have been appreciated."

She reached across the table and snagged a chicken leg from the enormous portion on his plate.

"Hey. No fair stealing."

A grin flashed just before her teeth sank into the meat and tore off a chunk.

"You think you can just pick up where you left off with swiping my food? You didn't even wait this time till I wasn't looking."

"You never minded sharing and you know it."

She was right. Unlike other girls, Paige had never been shy about taking what she wanted. She'd never been shy about eating in front of him. She'd never been shy about snatching a fry from his plate or even a bite of his cheeseburger. To his delight, on many occasions over the years, she had, in fact, turned eating into an erotic adventure.

Her tongue darted out to lick away a smear of sauce from her top lip, and his body went on full alert. During his deployments he fantasized about Paige. Her passion. The softness of her skin. The firmness of her breasts beneath his hands. The slick heat as he entered her body. During those long, lonely nights she'd become his dream girl. Sitting across from her now, watching her in the flesh, brought those fantasies back with a vengeance. Along with a sizeable erection.

For a moment they ate in silence. Then Paige set her fork down on her plate and folded her hands together. Because he knew her as well as he did, he predicted what she would say before the declarations were even out of her mouth. And like so many conversations they'd had in the past, he wanted to listen to every word. Not just to hear that sweet, sexy drawl, but because whatever she had to say was important.

"Aiden? I know you have a lot going on in your mind. I know you've been through more than most could ever even imagine. I won't tell you I understand. I won't say I know how you feel."

She reached across the table and covered his hand with her own. The contrast was startling. Hers small and soft. His large and calloused. The compassion in the gesture stole his breath. He'd forgotten the power of a tender touch. A gentle moment. A quiet calm that soothed a soul.

"What I will tell you," she continued, "is that I'm here for you. If you need to talk or even if you just need to sit and gaze out into the sky without a word. I'll be right here."

The pressure in his chest squeezed until he thought he might explode. She didn't know what she was saying. He had too much to tell—most of which was ugly and tragic. She was a soft, sweet woman who didn't need to hear all the hideous details of what he'd been through.

When you open yourself up to talk, it will help the nightmares go away.

The advice of his PTSD counselor sprang up inside his head. Before he could stomp it down, Aiden looked across the flicker of the votive candle into the eyes of the woman he'd known since she was a sprite in pigtails. He knew her. Trusted her. Believed she had a spine made of steel. And though he knew he had no business pulling her into his nightmare—knew he should just say what he'd come to say—if he wanted to talk to anyone about what had happened, Paige was the one.

"You sure about that?" he asked.

She gave him a slow nod.

In that moment, something greater than the fight-or-flee instinct took over. He took a long pull from his beer while the candlelight danced in her eyes. It wouldn't change what he'd come to tell her, but maybe the time had come for him to release the claws of anguish that had dug into his soul. And the only person he could imagine sharing that information with was Paige.

Chapter Four

LIKE THE SLOW release of pressure from a tea kettle, Paige listened to Aiden explain what had happened in Afghanistan. As they strolled along the bank of the creek, he told her of the local people and their small villages, many who only desired to exist and wanted to help the American soldiers. He told her of the Taliban who wanted no part in making peace. He told her nightmarish tales of men, women, and children being executed in the streets for no reason. And then he told her of the ambush. Their intel had been sketchy. The terrain rugged. And on that day he'd watched his two best friends die.

"There's not a waking moment that I don't think about those boys." He paused, ducked his head, and shook it slowly. "Boys. Hell. They were warriors. And I was honored to be their friend."

Paige pressed her hand against her chest to hold back the wail that threatened to push through. But she would not falter. Aiden trusted her to be strong. Perhaps this was the first time he'd chosen to recount his story. She would not and could not let him down.

He stopped beneath one of the more mature trees in the orchard—her favorite place to sit and think. Dream and desire. A place where she kept one of Aunt Bertie's handmade quilts wedged into a fork in the tree and the most recent romance novel she'd chosen to read tucked inside the quilt.

Aiden reached up and inspected a ripening Honeycrisp that dangled from a low branch. "And then . . . there was Rennie."

"Rennie?"

A smile pushed up the corners of his beautiful mouth, and Paige's heart stumbled.

"Renegade." He gave another slow shake of his head. "The fourth member of the three musketeers." When he looked up, his entire expression had changed from a simple smile to a full-on grin. "Intel was waiting for a break, and we had some rare down time. One night after dark, the boys and I headed into the tent for a game of cards. Billy had lost three games straight. In the midst of his complaints I heard a sound outside. When I went to check I found this . . . puppy. This little fluff of dirty golden fur wandering around outside our tent."

"A puppy?"

He nodded. "Wasn't unusual to see dogs or cats hanging around. Looking for food. Shelter. Someone to care. Needless to say, they don't view animals the same way over there as we do here."

His unspoken words sent a chill up her spine. She looked down at Cricket, who'd curled up at the base of the tree for a quick nap. Aiden didn't need to describe the neglect or abuse the animals there must suffer. And she couldn't bear to think of it.

"When I knelt down," Aiden continued, "that dirty little pup whimpered over to me. I picked him up. When he looked at me with those deep brown eyes and licked my chin, I was a goner." He laughed, and the genuine sound gave Paige hope.

"We weren't supposed to keep a pet. For a long time we hid him. Then when he got too big to hide, our commander—who'd known Rennie was there all along—just turned his head. When we had to go out in the field, someone else was willing to take care of Rennie while I was gone. He offered a lot of comfort to those of us who'd been away from home for so long. But when I'd come back, Rennie would be there. He never left my side."

A slow intake of air stuttered in his chest. "Until the day they sent me home and I had to leave him behind."

"Leave him behind?" The idea was unimaginable. "Why?"

"Not allowed."

"That's stupid."

"Pretty much."

The shadows that veiled his eyes told Paige all she needed to know. Leaving that dog behind had stripped him of anything else left in his soul.

She curled her fingers around his arm. "Isn't there something you can do?"

The broad, strong shoulders that bore the weight of so much grief lifted in a shrug. "Someone mentioned an organization that helps bring back soldier's dogs. But there are no guarantees."

"Oh, Aiden." She pulled him into her arms and embraced him. "I'm so sorry."

"I left him with my team." His hands settled lightly on her hips. "But all I can think about is him sitting there wondering why I abandoned him."

Paige's heart broke into a million pieces. Aiden was not the type of man to abandon anything or anyone. Though a poor dog alone in the middle of the desert wouldn't know that.

As water tumbled over the rocks in the creek and moved along the sand, Paige felt Aiden close himself off. Everything inside him seemed to be at war with the peaceful surroundings. As if he didn't deserve to be there. As if only a part of him stood on solid ground.

She pressed her cheek against his chest. Heard the stutter in his heart. She couldn't change what had happened. She could only offer him the chance to forget. If only for a moment.

Lifting her head, she looked up into the handsome face she'd known since before she'd learned to tie her shoes. While the moon glowed above them, a dragonfly skimmed the rippling waters, and the click-click of the cicadas surrounded them as they looked into each other's eyes.

Heat and tension pulled them together, and their lips touched on a brief kiss. He pressed his forehead against hers, and Paige curled her fingers around the back of his neck.

"I missed you," she whispered. "So much."

His dark gaze moved slowly over her face. The memories of lying in his arms, kissing him, tasting him, caught like a sigh in her chest. "Touch me, Aiden."

"My hands are dirty, Paige. I don't want—"

She knew that in his mind, he could never clean them enough to wash away what he'd had to do with them in the war. She stepped back. Instead of relief in his eyes, she saw sorrow. Hunger. Whatever battle raged within him, Paige knew she could give him the one thing he'd missed for God knew how long.

Comfort.

She grasped the bottom of her shirt and pulled it over her head. Then she reached between her breasts, unlatched the plain white cotton bra, and tossed it to the ground. She took a step forward until the tips of her breasts met with the smooth, worn cotton of his shirt.

"Touch me, Aiden." She let her fingertips waltz across his strong jawline. "Let me welcome you home like I've always dreamed."

How could he resist?

Good intentions told him to pick up her clothes and hand them back to her. Good intentions told him to walk away.

She deserved better.

Good intentions did *not* move lower in his body. Everything below his belt was running on heat, and emotion, and need. He'd loved Paige the day he'd tossed his duffel on his back and headed off to basic training. He'd loved her when his boots had hit the sands of Iraq. He'd loved her when he'd read her letters over and over—yet rarely responded.

For her sake.

He was responding now.

To her inner strength. Her optimism. Her unwillingness to give up on him.

For his sake.

Paige. The woman who'd waited for him. Even when there had been a significant chance he would never come home.

For weeks, months—hell, even years—he'd dreamed of holding her close. Touching her. Tasting her. Devouring her.

She deserved better than him.

Instead of walking away as he should, he curved his hands over her smooth shoulders, drew her close, and covered her mouth with his own. The soft touch of her lips brought him back. The womanly scent of her skin urged him to move forward and never look back. His hand slid down the curve of her spine, cupped her bottom, and brought her tight against his erection. She leaned into him, rose to the balls of her feet, and wrapped her arms around his neck with a sigh. His arms surrounded her and they came together—heart to heart. His gaze swept over her plump, moist mouth, and their lips met again. Their tongues touched and danced. And the past simply melted away. He could kiss her all day and it would never be enough.

Her fingers were cool as they slipped beneath his shirt to pull the fabric over his head. And then they stood flesh to flesh. Her body warm, ripe, and full of promise. Memories. Hope.

Desire burned inside of him as she briefly broke their embrace to grab a quilt stuck in the fork of the apple tree and spread it on the ground. And then she was back in his arms, touching him. Caressing him with heated silk that glided along his nerve endings, making his heart race, his desire spin out of control.

She unzipped his jeans and slid them down his legs. She tossed the pants into the increasing pile of clothes and kissed her way back up his thighs. Her long, delicate fingers embraced, stroked, and enticed his already throbbing erection. When she cupped him with gentle hands and took him into her mouth with a low hum of satisfaction, it was everything he could do not to buckle at his knees.

For a moment he stood there with his hands buried in the thick of her honey-gold hair, selfish with the need to feel whole again. Anxious with the desire to be one with her. To be buried deep within her warmth. To be held within her arms. He dropped to his knees, eased her back to the quilt, and followed her down. His hands molded to her full breasts, smoothed down her luscious curves. He bent his head and kissed her mouth, then he moved lower to savor the erect tips of her breasts. She tasted like sunshine, and honey, and all the good things he remembered about being alive.

When his heartbeat kicked into a frantic race, his hands made quick work of removing her jeans and tiny pink panties and adding them to the pile of clothes beneath the apple tree. Her warm, soft lips danced across his chest.

She looked up at him with a smile in her eyes. "I like your tattoo."

He gave a brief glance to the eagle in flight that covered his left bicep then leaned down and licked the small heart tattooed just above her left breast. "I like yours too."

He moved over her, their bodies pressed together, and she opened to let him in. He slid inside her and was overcome by the rush of liquid heat. He lowered his forehead to hers until he could quell the need to pump hard and find a fast release. When his mind finally got the signal, they settled into slow, languid movements that allowed him to soak in every tiny sensation that spiraled through their connected bodies.

"I'm so glad you're home," she sighed against his ear.

For the moment, he was glad too.

Before his demons returned to mess with his thoughts, he gave Paige all his attention. He made slow, sweet love to her, as if he were still the man he used to be. When they came together with a final thrust and moan, Aiden realized that he'd give anything to be the man Paige wanted him—needed him—to be.

As much as he wanted it to be true, he also realized it was impossible to resurrect the dead.

Chapter Five

CONTENT AND SATED in Aiden's arms, Paige knew the exact moment his past came crashing down. His body suddenly tensed at noises that had surrounded them the entire night. Yet now, he reacted as if they were the enemy. Oh, he wasn't *showing* her any of that, but when you knew the boy before he'd become the man, it wasn't hard to see. Her only alternative became distraction.

She rolled to her side and laid her head on his shoulder. Then she took advantage of his perfect, masculine chest and let her fingers play in the soft, fine hair. "We can do that again anytime you're ready."

To her delight, he chuckled.

"I've been out of commission for so long, recovery could go either way."

"Mmmm." She leaned in and kissed him. "I'm willing to wait."

In that moment, his body tensed in a whole different way. And though she tried to drag her arm across him to hold him in place, she did not succeed. Before she could mutter the words "What are you doing?" he was up and tugging on his clothes.

Damn.

"What's the hurry?" she asked.

His hands stopped on his jeans mid-zip. He watched her through eyes filled with regret.

Damn it.

"I'm sorry, Paige."

"Don't say that." When she realized he wasn't going to come back and lie down beside her, she felt exposed and got up to dress. "There's nothing to be sorry for."

"The hell there isn't." The zipper on his jeans slid to the top, and he shook that old grey T-shirt like a flag of surrender. "I just took advantage of you."

"Are you crazy?" She yanked her T-shirt over her head. "I'm no Strawberry Shortcake, Aiden. I wanted you. You wanted me. That's consensual need. *Not* exploitation."

"I shouldn't have done that."

"You beautiful fool." A humorless laugh pushed past her lips. She looked up at him through the moonlight. "I've waited years for you to do exactly *that*."

He jammed his fingers into his short hair then dropped his hands to his lean hips. "I didn't come see you today for this, Paige."

"I know." She folded her arms across her chest as if they could hold back all the emotions. All the things she wanted to say.

"I came . . . to tell you goodbye," he said. His tone quiet. His words flat.

Her heart slammed against her ribs. "You're leaving again?"

"I don't know." He glanced behind him, then back at her. "I don't know what the hell I'm doing. I'm broken, Paige. And I'm pretty damned sure nothing can fix me."

"That's bull."

He shook his head. "The person you knew went to war and never came back. You deserve better than what I have to give."

"The man I *knew* is standing right here. Feeding me a bunch of crap I don't believe."

"Move on, Paige. Forget about me." He glanced away again, and Paige knew even he was having a hard time believing his own words. Then those dark, haunted eyes came right back to her. "I can't love you."

"Can't? Or don't?" She sucked in a lungful of air to calm the desperation churning like butter in her stomach. "Because there's a difference."

His chin dropped to his chest and he shook his head. "Too much has happened."

"Maybe so. But you're wrong, Aiden. You're still the man you used to be. Only more." Paige kept her voice calm. Yelling wouldn't get through to him. He had to arrive at conclusions on his own. No amount of whining or persuading would do a bit of good. She just had to state the facts and then give him time. She'd already given him plenty. What were a few more days, weeks, months?

"I love you, Aiden." The confession that jumped from her mouth was not a surprise to either of them. "I always have. If I have to give you up because you've fallen in love with someone else, I'll do it. I won't like it, but I'll do it. Because your happiness means everything to me." Her fingers curled into her palms. "But I will *not* give you up and let this sorrow swallow you and make you disappear. I can't do that."

She slowly shook her head and held back the wash of tears that burned in her eyes. "*You* may have given up on you. But I *never* will."

Several heartbeats passed while they stood an arm's length away from each other in a stare-down that Paige swore she would win. At their feet Cricket woke from her nap and gave a little whine as if she sensed the tension in the air. Paige stood in place, resolute that she would not bend in her belief. No matter what he said.

The pressure in her chest squeezed harder as he bent at the knees and gave Cricket a brisk rub on her head. Then he stood, stepped forward, and wrapped Paige in his arms. He held her tight. Kissed her forehead. And completely broke her heart.

"Goodbye, Paige."

Chapter Six

IF YOU WANTED to get the word out in Sweet, one method worked faster than picking up the phone. Luckily for Paige, today the Digging Divas Garden Club held their monthly meeting at Bud's Diner. In two shakes of a can of whipped cream, the message would go out faster than a speedboat on smooth water.

Paige grabbed her keys off Aunt Bertie's oak dresser and jogged down the stairs. Just like when she'd gone for her college degree or made the purchase of Honey Hill, she had a plan. So far she'd been batting a thousand. She wouldn't allow this goal to be any different. It simply meant too much.

Ten minutes later her red F-150 slid to a gravel-spewing-stop in the lot beside Bud's. She grabbed her work apron from the seat and jumped down from the truck. The lot was still half-full with late morning coffee-slurpers. In another hour the lunch crowd would converge and there would be standing room only. A perfect audience for when she sounded the alarm.

"I STAYED UP HALF the night doing Internet research," Paige said, searching the focused expressions around the crowded tables. Her heart trembled with how much they cared about the situation and how eager they were to help. "Early this morning I made a few calls to the organization and they said they would look into it. Well, they work fast. Before I left for work they called me back with the news that they can make it happen. They don't require a fee, but they do ask for donations to keep them afloat and able to help others in the same situation. I figure we need to come in around four thousand."

"Dollars?" The brim of Ethel Weber's lime green straw hat bobbled above her lavender hair.

"Hard, cold, American cash," Paige answered.

"That's nothing." Ray Calhoun lifted his old farmer's hand in a dismissive wave. "Hell, we raised ten thousand to pay for Missy Everhart's funeral when she took ill so fast."

"Can't put a dollar amount on what this will do for someone who's given so much," said Jan West, owner of Goody Gum Drops, the candy store painted like a peppermint stick in the center of town.

"Can we get it done before the Apple Butter Festival?" Paige asked the crowd gathered inside the diner.

"Three weeks?" Hazel Calhoun scoffed. "Easy Cheesy."

Bill McBride, Vietnam vet and local good guy, stood,

imposing in his leather vest and various military patches. "Consider it done." He turned to the crowd. "Right?"

The unity in the agreement that echoed across the diner sent a ribbon of warmth fluttering through Paige's heart.

Aiden may not ask for much, but the people who loved him the most were about to give him everything.

THE AXE ARCED high overhead then slammed into the rotted tree trunk. Aiden pulled his hands back, yanked a bandana from his back pocket, and swept the cloth across his forehead.

Damn the sun was hot today.

He'd promised his brother, Ben, that until he figured out what the hell to do with his life, he'd help out around the farm and orchard. At the rate he was going he didn't imagine he'd figure it out any time soon.

It had been nearly two weeks since he'd walked out of Paige's life. Two weeks since he'd slept little more than a couple of hours without dreaming of her. Two weeks in which his instincts had screamed for him to get his stupid ass back in his truck and go to her. Take her in his arms. And beg her forgiveness. He wrapped his hands around the axe handle and dislodged the wedge from the tree stump. But his instincts had been wrong before. They'd even gotten his two best friends killed. So what the hell did he know?

Not to trust himself. That was what.

"Thought you'd be long gone by now."

Mid-swing, he looked up, surprised to see Paige and her dog coming toward him. Damn. The woman managed to make a pair of jean shorts and a silky little tank top look hotter than some flimsy piece of lingerie. Her hair was pulled up into a just-out-of-bed tangle on top of her head and her smooth skin was kissed with a golden tan. While her white tennis shoes ate up the ground, her tongue darted out to lick the half-eaten cherry Popsicle in her hand. The heat rolling through his body had nothing to do with the sun above his head.

"Yeah. Me too," he said as Cricket plopped her furry dog butt in the shade of a nearby tree.

Bringing with her the scent of ripe peaches, Paige came to a stop in front of him. "So why are you still here?"

How could he explain that while he didn't quite know where he belonged, he also couldn't bear the thought of never seeing her again? That he couldn't bring himself to just pick up and walk away. A lump lodged in his throat as he thought of Rennie. He'd unwillingly walked away from the dog who'd given him companionship and loyalty. Did he really believe he could *willingly* walk away from Paige?

He shrugged and felt the sting of a sunburn on his shoulders. "Promised Ben I'd help him out."

Her red-stained tongue licked up the side of the Popsicle while she studied him through those sharp blue eyes—which triggered an instant reaction in his jeans. Her head tilted. "Is that so?"

"Yep."

"I'm sure Ben appreciates your help."

"What are you doing here?" he asked, although he didn't mind having her in front of him with next to nothing on, licking that Popsicle like it was . . . tasty.

She smiled and tossed the remainder of the Popsicle to Cricket. Then she turned those blue eyes on him. "I've come to make you a proposition."

A LAYER OF SWEAT glistened across the tops of Aiden's broad, strong shoulders. Highlighted that soaring eagle tattoo. Beaded down his chest and rippled stomach toward the waistband of his low-slung Levi's. Unlike the thugs one saw walking the streets of the big city, Aiden did not have a mile of underwear showing. Which only made Paige wonder if he had any on at all or if he'd gone commando. A blue bandana stuck out from his back pocket, and his work boots had a coating of sawdust across the toes.

A low hum vibrated low in her pelvis. There was just something about a shirtless, sweaty, hard-working man that made her want to tear off her clothes. When that hard-working man was as gorgeous and amazing as Aiden, it was a wonder she hadn't given in to the desire. It took everything she had to compose herself and stick to what she'd come here for in the first place. Which did not include gawking at him or being tempted to stick dollar bills in his shorts.

"A proposition?" A furrow crinkled between his brown eyes.

"Not *that* kind of proposition." Although it had

crossed her mind. "I'm going to respect what you said the other night even though I don't agree. Are you willing to listen to my offer?"

He leaned the axe handle against the tree trunk he'd been chopping and folded his arms across that amazing, muscular, sweaty chest. "Shoot."

She hopped up on the tailgate of his truck. "When I made the decision to buy Honey Hill I knew I couldn't have that much property or responsibility without a good business plan. And . . ." She swung her legs back and forth in time with the thoughts swinging through her brain. "I might have dreamed a little too big."

"Are you afraid of losing the place?"

"Oh. No. Nothing like that." The concern on his face forced her to quit stalling. "Part of my plan is to expand the orchard. Instead of just trying to sell apples, I plan to create apple products—butter, jelly, cider. That kind of thing. I need to do more research. Crunch some more numbers. Come up with a marketing plan. And—"

"And?" Dark eyebrows shot up his forehead. "That's not enough?"

"Oh, you know me. Complete one project, come up with ten more."

"I do remember that about you."

The smile and slow glide of his eyes over her body said that wasn't all he remembered.

"And I plan to turn the house into a bed-and-breakfast."

"Wow. You are ambitious." He laughed. "But what has this got to do with me?"

"Both my sisters have their own thing going on. And I need a partner." She hopped down from the tailgate. "You interested?"

"I'm a soldier, Paige. What do I know about cider and bed-and-breakfasts?"

"You're smart. You know apples. You're handy with tools. And people love you."

He shook his head. "Not true."

"*Never* disregard the way people feel about you, Aiden. Sometimes . . . it's all you have."

His head came up and something sparked in his eyes that gave her the smallest pinch of hope.

"You don't have to give me an answer right now. Just think about it." She gave a whistle to Cricket who reluctantly got up from her cool spot beneath the tree. Paige felt the heat of Aiden's gaze on her backside as she walked toward her truck. Someday he'd trust his instincts. His gut. His heart. And he'd let life happen. Until then she'd wait. Apparently she'd become quite good at that.

"Why are you doing this, Paige?"

She turned at the sound of his deep voice, inhaled one more glimpse of that mouthwatering physique, and noted the look of complete and utter puzzlement on his face.

"We're a good team, Aiden." She lifted her hands in the air then dropped them with a slap against her thighs. "Maybe someday you'll figure that out."

Chapter Seven

A WEEK LATER, AIDEN stepped from the shower, wrapped a towel around his waist, and went in search of something decent to wear that didn't say camo or thread-bare cotton. Five days ago he'd been cornered in the cereal aisle of the Touch and Go Market by Gladys Lewis and Arlene Potter, president and co-president of the Sweet Apple Butter Festival committee. After they charmed him with compliments on his cereal choice—Cap'n Crunch original, not Crunch Berries—and thanked him for his service in the Army, they'd asked him to be a judge in the festival's apple butter competition. Apparently the prior year there had been a controversy due to favoritism.

How could he refuse the two little blue-hairs? Especially when, mid-sentence, Gladys turned around and smeared a glob of crimson lipstick across her mouth so she'd look pretty for a soldier like him. Or so she said. So now, when he'd rather be enjoying the festivities from where he could blend into the background, he'd be thrust in the spotlight. With respect he would listen to all the nice things people had to say, while deep inside he thought of himself as a total screw-up. He'd failed his best friends. He'd abandoned his dog. And he'd disappointed Paige.

Jesus. He was batting a thousand.

He turned his attention back to matters he could control. There were two sides of clothing choices in his closet. Military and ultra-casual. Not much in-between. He grabbed a freshly laundered button-down shirt off a hanger and jammed his legs through a pair of khakis he'd swiped from Ben's closet. A split second later he grabbed his keys, headed toward his truck, and prayed he would not be accused of favoritism if Paige had entered the contest this year.

A WIDE VARIETY OF SUVs, trucks, and economy cars were parked bumper-to-bumper along the curb at the Town Square—better known as the entertainment hub of Sweet. Whether it was a birthday party, a battle of the bands, or the Fourth of July picnic, it happened in the little park smack dab in the center of town. Though the latticework gazebo had seen better days and the trees were tall and ancient, the folks mingling around the grass lot filled the square with spirit and a sense of renewal.

Aiden glanced past the rainbow of canopies where vendors hawked everything from scented candles to homemade cinnamon rolls to handmade animal pup-

pets. Over the brims of sun-deflecting Stetsons and ball-
caps he scanned the area to find the banner that would
lead him toward the judging area. He finally spotted it
toward the gazebo where someone on the loud speaker
called out the winner of the cake-walk. The huge crowd
gathered in front of the area made him wonder if he
might be late. A quick glance at his watch said he was
right on time. As he started toward the crowd, the two
charmers who'd conned him into the gig appeared like
magician's assistants.

"My, don't you look handsome," Gladys Lewis said
through wrinkly lips smeared with carnation pink.

"We thought you might have worn your uniform,"
Arlene Potter commented, giving him a questionable
once-over.

"I apologize, ladies. I'm no longer a member of the
military."

"Good Lord." Gladys gave her cohort a whack with
her lace fan. "You knew that, Arlene."

"I'm sorry."

Not wanting to cause the elderly women to feel uncomfortable, Aiden flashed them both a smile.

"Too bad, though," Arlene added with a wink. "Nothing hotter than a man in uniform."

"Good heavens." Gladys rolled her faded blue eyes.
"Come on, young man. Pay no attention to her. She's just
getting old, and her marbles don't always roll in the same
direction."

The women in their floral dresses and straw hats
hooked their arms through his and led him through the

crowd. As they drew closer to the gazebo, the festival attendees turned toward them and began to part like a gaping zipper. The whole scene felt odd and a prickle of alarm crept up the back of his neck. Had it not been for the friendly faces turned his way, he may very well have made a beeline in another direction.

"It's okay, Lieutenant." Gladys gave him a light pat on his arm. He looked down into the reassuring smile on her weathered face. "We're just glad to have you home." She gave a nod toward the gazebo. "Some of us more than others."

When Aiden looked up he saw Paige in a floaty yellow sundress. Her hair had been pulled back in a long braid, tousled by the summer breeze. Her beautiful mouth lifted at the corners. Aiden swore he'd never seen anything prettier in his life. As she held her hand out for him to join her, his heart went warm and fuzzy.

Gladys and Arlene blended back into the crowd, and he took a few steps forward. It was then he realized Paige wasn't reaching out to him. She was letting go of a yellow ribbon that slowly fluttered toward the ground. His gaze followed the ribbon down to the green grass and the large golden dog who sat back on his haunches like the most patient soldier.

Aiden's heart leaped into his throat, and the ever-present ache in his chest disappeared. In a rush of disbelief, he dropped to his knees.

"Rennie!"

The retriever's massive paws dug into the earth, and within a warm flash of sunshine Aiden had his arms around his friend's soft, silky neck. Rennie whined and wiggled and did a doggy happy dance. If dogs could smile, Rennie had a full-on grin. Aiden did, too, as Rennie's long tongue slurped up the side of his face.

"I've missed you, boy."

Aiden thought of all the nights he'd shared his cot with a scared little pup. One who'd grown so big Aiden had considered sleeping on the ground when that cot became too small for the both of them. They'd seen hell together. Shared sorrow. They'd even shared meals. He gave the dog a kiss on the top of his head and laughed at the exultant bark he received in response. With another lick to Aiden's face, Rennie flopped down on his side and rolled over for a shameless belly rub.

Forgiven.

Just like that Rennie forgave him.

Aiden curled his fingers in the dog's thick fur and did his best to hide the tears swimming in his eyes. When he looked up, Paige came toward him with Cricket prancing on a leash by her side.

Paige looked at him with those blue eyes and smiled. "Welcome home, Lieutenant Marshall."

"Welcome home," the rest of his community cheered.

If there had ever been any doubt of where Aiden belonged or who he belonged to or with, it dissipated right then and there.

He stood. "How did you find him?"

"*We* found him," she said, "Eagerly waiting to be brought home to you."

"*We?*"

She gave a nod to those surrounding them. "Sweet. All

the people you went off to protect. All the people who've been waiting to welcome you home. They all came together and made this happen . . . because they know how much you love this dog. And because they love you." She tilted her head back and smiled. "Of course, not nearly as much as I do."

A smile burst from his heart as he looked at the faces surrounding him. "I don't know how to thank you. Or how to repay you."

"You owe us nothing in return, Lieutenant Marshall," Bill McBride returned. "You've paid your dues. Just be happy."

Aiden curled his fingers in Rennie's thick fur, wrapped his arm around Paige, and gave the Vietnam vet who'd seen plenty during his own tour-of-duty a nod. "I'll do what I can."

Paige flashed him a smile then turned it toward the crowd. "All right. Y'all have seen enough. Judging starts in thirty minutes."

As the crowd slowly dispersed, Aiden shook his head. "Do they always mind you like that?"

"If they want fresh pickles and crunchy lettuce on their burgers, they do."

He smiled, gazed down into the passion and comfort in her eyes, and brushed a long tendril of honey-gold hair away from her face. His friends—better men than he— had not made it back home. He would not dishonor their memories by taking life and all it offered for granted. He was grateful to have an opportunity to love Paige for the rest of his life. And there was no time like the present to make that happen. *If* she'd still have him.

"I'm in," he said.

Her soft golden brows pulled together. "In?"

"The partnership. I'm taking you up on your offer, if it's still on the table."

"Of course it is."

"Good." He tugged her closer. "Then I accept. On two conditions."

"Which are?"

"I pay my half up front. Equal partners."

"That's one condition." Her hand slid up to his shoulder. "What's the other?"

"We make it permanent."

She leaned her head back as though he'd offended her. "I would never offer you half the business if I didn't expect it to be long-term."

"Not the business. You and me." He lowered his mouth to hers—not caring if they had an audience or if the whole world watched—and he kissed her with everything he felt in his heart. "We're a good team."

"Yes. We are." Her warm fingers caressed the side of his face. "You know, you're quite the negotiator. Maybe you should think about running for mayor in the fall."

"Mayor?"

"Why not?" The music of her laughter danced across his skin. "You've proven to be quite a service-oriented kind of guy. Running the town should be easy after what you've been through."

He nuzzled her sweet-scented neck. "I might be too busy."

"You keep that up and I guarantee you *will* be too busy."

A playful bark interrupted them and they both looked down to where Rennie was busy snuffling Cricket's ear.

"Looks like Rennie's quite at home here." Paige laughed. "He might have even found love."

"He's not the only one." Aiden caught Paige's hand in his and kissed her fingers. "*You're* home to me. And while I may never be the man I was before I left here—"

She pressed a finger to his lips. "That's okay. I'm not the same woman."

No she wasn't. She was more. More than he ever expected. More than he deserved. She was a gift he'd treasure always.

"I love you, Paige. I always have. And I want to be with you for the rest of my life." He gave her hand a squeeze. "Say yes."

"It's always been yes, Aiden." She lifted to her toes, wrapped her arms around his neck, and kissed him. "Always."

Author's Note

THE INSPIRATION FOR *Home Sweet Home* came from an article I read about Nowzad—a charity set up to relieve the suffering of dogs, cats, and even donkeys in Afghanistan. They provide and maintain rescue facilities for the care and treatment of these animals. I read the many rescue/reunion stories they have on their website, and my heart was deeply touched. For more information please check out their website at http://www.nowzad.com and donate if you can.

If you loved *Home Sweet Home*
and want more from the wonderful Candis Terry,
continue reading for an excerpt from
SECOND CHANCE AT THE SUGAR SHACK,
the first in her sexy, funny, and oh-so-delicious
Sugar Shack series . . .
Available from Avon Books wherever e-books are sold

Kate Silver's back in town, and her dead mother just won't leave her alone.

Kate usually spends her days dressing Hollywood A-listers, but after her estranged mother dies she finds herself elbow-deep in flour in her parents' bakery . . . in Deer Lick, Montana. She thought she'd left small-town life far, far behind, but it seems there are a few loose ends.

The boy she once loved, Deputy Matt Ryan, is single and sexy and still has a thing for her . . . and handcuffs.

Her mother, who won't follow the white light, is determined to give maternal advice from beyond the grave.

And somehow Kate's three-day stay has, well . . . extended. She never planned to fill her mother's pie-baking shoes—she prefers her Choos thank you very much. But with the help of a certain man in uniform, Kate quickly learns that sometimes second chances are all the more sweet.

Chapter One

KATE SILVER HAD five minutes. Tops.

Five minutes before her fashion schizophrenic client had a meltdown.

Five minutes before her career rocketed into the bargain basement of media hell.

Behind the gates of one of the trendiest homes in the Hollywood Hills, Kate dropped to her hands and knees in a crowded bedroom *In Style* magazine had deemed "Wacky Tacky." Amid the dust bunnies and cat hair clinging for life to a faux zebra rug, she crawled toward her most current disaster—repairing the Swarovski crystals ripped from the leather pants being worn by pop music's newly crowned princess.

Gone was the hey-day of Britney, Christina, and Shakira.

Long live *Inara*.

Why women in pop music never had a last name was

a bizarre phenomenon Kate didn't have time to ponder. At the end of the day, the women she claimed as clients didn't need a last name to be at the top of her V.I.P. list. They didn't need one when they thanked her—their stylist—from the red carpet. And they certainly didn't need one when they signed all those lovely zeros on her paychecks.

Right now she sat in chaos central, earning every penny. Awards season had arrived and her adrenaline had kicked into overdrive alongside the triple-shot latte she'd sucked down for lunch. Over the years she'd become numb to the mayhem. Even so, she did enjoy the new talent—of playing Henry Higgins to the Eliza Doolittles and Huck Finns of Tinsel Town. Nothing compared to the rush she got from seeing her babies step onto a stage and sparkle. The entire process made her feel proud and accomplished.

It made her feel necessary.

Surrounded by the gifted artists who lifted their fairy dusted makeup brushes and hair extensions, Kate brushed a clump of floating cat hair from her nose. Why the star getting all the attention had yet to hire a housekeeper was anyone's guess. Regardless, Kate intended to keep the current catastrophe from turning into the Nightmare on Mulholland Drive.

Adrenaline slammed into her chest and squeezed the air from her lungs.

This was her job. She'd banked all her worth into what she did and she was damn good at it. No matter how crazy it made her. No matter how much it took over her life.

After her triumph on the Oscars red carpet three years ago, she'd become the stylist the biggest names in Hollywood demanded. Finally. She'd become an overnight sensation that had only taken her seven long years to achieve. And though there were times she wanted to stuff a feather boa down some snippy starlet's windpipe, she now had to fight to maintain her success. Other stylists, waiting for their star to shine, would die for what she had. On days like today, she would willingly hand it over.

In the distance the doorbell chimed and Kate's five minutes shrank to nada. The stretch limo had arrived to deliver Inara to the Nokia Theatre for the televised music awards. With no time to spare, Kate plunged the needle through the leather and back up again. Her fingers moved so fast blisters formed beneath the pressure.

Peggy Miller, Inara's agent, paced the floor and sidestepped the snow-white animal shelter refugee plopped in the middle of a leopard rug. Clearly the cat wasn't intimidated by the agent's nicotine-polluted voice.

"Can't you hurry that up, Kate?" Peggy tapped the Cartier on her wrist with a dragon nail. "Inara's arrival has to be timed perfectly. Not enough to dawdle in the interviews and just enough to make the media clamor for more. Sorry, darling," she said to Inara, "chatting with the media is just not your strong point."

Inara made a hand gesture that was far from the bubble gum persona everyone in the industry tried to portray with the new star. Which, in Kate's estimation, was like fitting a square peg into a round hole.

"Kate?" Peggy again. "Hurry!"

"I'm working on it," Kate mumbled around the straight pins clenched between her teeth. Just her luck their wayward client had tried to modify the design with a fingernail file and pair of tweezers an hour before showtime.

"Why do I have to wear this . . . thing." Inara tugged the embossed leather tunic away from her recently enhanced bustline. "It's hideous."

The needle jabbed Kate's thumb. She flinched and bit back the slur that threatened to shoot from her mouth. "Impossible," she said. "It's Armani." And to acquire it she'd broken two fingernails wrestling another stylist to the showroom floor. She'd be damned if she'd let the singer out the door without wearing it now.

"Inara, please hold still," the makeup artist pleaded while she attempted to dust bronzer on her moving target.

"More teasing in back?" the hair stylist asked.

Kate flicked a gaze up to Inara's blond hair extensions. "No. We want her to look sultry. Not like a streetwalker."

"My hair color is all wrong," Inara announced. "I want it more like yours, Kate. Kind of a ritzy porn queen auburn." She ran her manicured fingers through the top of Kate's hair, lifting a few strands. "And I love these honey-colored streaks."

"Thanks," Kate muttered without looking up. "I think." Her hair color had been compared to many things. A ritzy porn queen had never been one of them.

"Hmmm. I will admit, these pants seriously make my ass rock," Inara said, changing gears with a glance over her shoulder to the cheval mirror. "But this vest . . . I don't know. I really think I should wear my red sequin tube top instead."

Kate yanked the pins from her between her teeth. "You can *not* wear a *Blue Light Special* with Armani. It's a sin against God." Kate blinked hard to ward off the migraine that poked between her eyes. "Besides, the last time you made a last-minute fashion change you nearly killed my career."

"I didn't mean to. It's just . . . God, Kate, you are so freaking strict with this fashion crap. It's like having my mother threaten to lower the hem on my school uniform."

"You pay me to threaten you. Remember?"

"I pay you plenty."

"Then trust me plenty." Kate wished the star would do exactly that. "Once those lights hit these crystals, all the attention will be on you. You're up for the new artist award. You should shine. You don't want to end up a fashion tragedy like the time Sharon Stone wore a Gap turtleneck to the Oscars, do you?"

"No."

"Good. Because that pretty much ended her career."

Inara's heavily made-up eyes widened. "A shirt did that?"

"Easier to blame it on a bad garment choice than bad acting."

"Oh."

"Kate? Do you want the hazelnut lipstick?" the makeup artist asked. "Or the caramel gloss?"

Kate glanced between the tubes. "Neither. Use the Peach Shimmer. It will play up her eyes. And make sure she takes it with her. She'll need to reapply just before they announce her category and the cameras go for the close-up."

"Kate!" Peggy again. "You have got to hustle. The traffic on Sunset will be a nightmare."

Kate wished for superpowers, wished for her fingers to work faster, wished she could get the job done and Inara in the limo. She needed Inara to look breathtaking when she stepped onto that red carpet. She needed a night full of praise for the star, the outfit, *and* the stylist.

Scratch that. It was not just a need, it was absolutely critical.

Inara's past two public appearances had been disasters. One had been Kate's own oversight—the canary and fuchsia Betsey Johnson had looked horrible under the camera lights. She should have known that before sending her client out for the fashion wolves to devour. The second calamity hadn't been her fault, but had still reflected on her. That time had been cause and effect of a pop royalty temper tantrum and Inara's fondness for discount store castoffs. It may have once worked for Madonna, but those days were locked in the fashion vault. For a reason.

Kate couldn't afford to be careless again. And she couldn't trust the bubble gum diva to ignore the thrift store temptations schlepping through her blood. Not that there was anything wrong with that for ordinary people. Inara did not fall into the *ordinary* category.

Not anymore.

Not if Kate could help it.

As soon as she tied off the last stitch, she planned to escort her newest client right into the backseat of the limo with a warning to the driver to steer clear of all second-hand clothing establishments along the way.

"This totally blows." Inara slid the shears from the table and aimed them at the modest neckline. "It's just not sexy enough."

"Stop that!" Kate's heart stopped. She grabbed the scissors and tucked them beneath her knee. "Tonight is not about selling sex. Leave that for your music videos. Tonight is about presentation. Wowing the critics. Tomorrow you want to end up on the best-dressed list. Not the *What the hell was she thinking?* list."

Inara sighed. "Whatever."

"And don't pout," Kate warned. *Or be so ungrateful.* "It will mess up your lip liner."

"How's this look?" the makeup artist asked, lifting the bronzer away from one last dusting of Inara's forehead.

Kate glanced up mid-stitch. "Perfect. Now, everybody back away and let me get this last crystal on."

"Kate!"

"I know, Peggy. I know!"

Kate grasped the leather pant leg to keep Inara from checking out the junk in her trunk again via the full-length mirror. She shifted on her knees. A collection of cat hair followed.

Once she had Inara en route, Kate planned to rush home and watch the red carpet arrivals on TV. Alone. Collapsed on her sofa with a bag of microwave popcorn and a bottle of Moët. If the night went well, the celebration cork would fly. If not, well, tomorrow morning she'd have to place a *Stylist for Hire—Cheap* ad in *Variety*.

Kate pushed the needle through the leather, ignoring the hurried, sloppy stitches. If her mother could see her now, she'd cringe at the uneven, wobbly lengths. Then she'd deliver a pithy lecture on why a career in Hollywood was not right for Kate. Neither the Girl Scout sewing badge she'd earned as a kid nor the fashion award she'd recently won would ever be enough to stop her mother from slicing and dicing her dreams.

Her chest tightened.

God, how long had it been since she'd even talked to her mother? Easter? The obligatory Mother's Day call?

In her mother's eyes, Kate would never win the daughter-of-the-year award. She'd quit trying when she hit the age of thirteen—the year she'd traded in her 4-H handbook for a *Vogue* magazine.

Her mother had never forgiven her.

For two long years after high school graduation, there had been a lull in Kate's life while she waited anxiously for acceptance and a full scholarship to the design school in Los Angeles. Two years of her mother nagging at her to get a traditional college degree. Two years of working alongside her parents in their family bakery, decorating cakes with the same boring buttercream roses, pounding out the same tasteless loaves of bread. Not that she minded the work. It gave her a creative outlet. If only her mother had let her shake things up a little with an occasional fondant design or something that tossed a challenge her way.

Then the letter of acceptance arrived.

Kate had been ecstatic to show it to her parents. She knew her mother wouldn't be happy or supportive. But she'd never expected her mother to tell her that the best thing Kate could do would be to tear up the scholarship and stop wasting time. The argument that ensued had led to tears and hateful words. That night Kate made a decision that would forever change her life.

It had been ten years since she'd left her mother's unwelcome advice and small-town life in the dust. Without a word to anyone she'd taken a bus ride and disappeared. Her anger had faded over the years, but she'd never mended the damage done by her leaving. And she'd never been able to bring herself to come home. She'd met up with her parents during those years, but it had always been on neutral ground. Never in her mother's backyard. Despite her mother's reservations, Kate had grown up and become successful.

She slipped the needle through the back of the bead cap and through the leather again. As much as she tried to ignore it, the pain caused by her mother's disapproval still hurt.

Amid the boom-boom-boom of Snoop Dog on the stereo and Peggy's non-stop bitching, Kate's cell phone rang.

"Do *not* answer that," Peggy warned.

"It might be important. I sent Josh to Malibu." Dressing country music's top male vocalist was an easy gig for her assistant. He'd survived three awards seasons by her side. He could walk the tightrope with the best of them.

But as Kate well knew, trouble could brew and usually did.

Ignoring the agent's evil glare, Kate scooted toward her purse, grabbed her phone and shoved it between her ear and shoulder. Her fingers continued to stitch.

"Josh, what's up?"

"Katie?"

Whoa. Her heart did a funny flip that stole her breath. *Definitely not Josh.*

"Dad. Uh . . . hi. I . . . haven't talked to you in, uh . . ." *Forever.* "What's up?"

"Sweetheart, I . . . I don't know how to say this."

The hitch in his tone was peculiar. The sewing needle between her fingers froze midair. "Dad? Are you okay?"

"I'm . . . afraid not, honey." He released a breathy sigh. "I know it's asking a lot but . . . I wondered . . . could you come home?"

Her heart thudded to a halt. "What's wrong?"

"Katie, this morning . . . your mother died."

Chapter Two

A HUNDRED MILES OF heifers, hay fields, and rolling hills zipped past while Kate stared out the passenger window of her mother's ancient Buick. The flight from L.A. hadn't been long, but from the moment she'd received her father's call the day before, the tension hadn't uncurled from her body. The hour and a half drive from the *local* airport hadn't helped.

With her sister, Kelly, behind the wheel, they eked out the final miles toward home. Or what had been her home a lifetime ago.

They traveled past the big backhoe where the Dudley Brothers Excavation sign proclaimed: We dig our job! Around the curve came the Beaver Family Dairy Farm where a familiar stench wafted through the air vents. As they cruised by, a big Holstein near the fence lifted its tail.

"Eeew." Kelly wrinkled her nose. "Gross."

Kate dropped her head back to the duct-taped seat

and closed her eyes. "I'll never look at guacamole the same again."

"Yeah. Quite a welcome home." Her sister peered at her through a pair of last season Coach sunglasses. With her ivory blond hair caught up in a haphazard ponytail, she looked more like a frivolous teen than a fierce prosecutor. "It's funny. You move away from the Wild Wild West, buy your beef in Styrofoam packages, and forget where that hamburger comes from."

"Kel, nobody eats Holsteins. They're milk cows."

"I know. I'm just saying."

Whatever she was saying, she wasn't actually saying. It wasn't the first time Kate had to guess what was going on in her big sister's beautiful head. Being a prosecutor had taught Kelly to be tight-lipped and guarded. Though they were only two years apart in age, a world of difference existed in their personalities and style. Kelly had always been on the quiet side. She'd always had her nose stuck in a book, was always the type to smooth her hand over a wrinkled cushion just to make it right. Always the type to get straight A's and still worry she hadn't studied enough.

Kate took a deep breath and let it out slowly.

It was hard to compete with perfection like that.

"I still can't believe it's been ten years since you've been home," Kelly said.

Kate frowned as they passed the McGruber farm where someone had planted yellow mums in an old toilet placed on the front lawn. "And now I get the pleasure of remembering why I left in the first place."

"I don't know." Kelly leaned forward and peered through the pitted windshield. "It's really spectacular in an unrefined kind of way. The fall colors are on parade and snow is frosting the mountain peaks. Chicago might be beautiful, but it doesn't compare to this." Lines of concern scrunched between Kelly's eyes ruined the perfection of her face. "I know how hard this is for you, Kate. But I'm glad you came."

The muscles between Kate's shoulders tightened. Right now, she didn't want to think about what might be difficult for her. Others were far more important. "I'm here for Dad," she said.

"You know, I was thinking the other day . . . we all haven't been together since we met up at the Super Bowl last year." Kelly shook her head and smiled. "God. No matter that our brother was playing, I thought you and Mom were going to root for opposing teams just so you'd have one more thing to disagree about."

"I did not purposely spill my beer on her."

Kelly laughed. "Yes, you did."

The memory came back in full color and Kate wanted to laugh too.

"That's why Dad will be really glad to see you, Kate. You've always made him smile. You know you were always his favorite."

At least she'd been *somebody's* favorite. "I've missed him." Kate fidgeted with the string attached to her hoodie. "I didn't mean to . . ."

"I know." Kelly wrapped her fingers around the steering wheel. "He knew too."

The reminder of her actions stuck in Kate's throat. If she could do it all over, she'd handle it much differently. At the time she'd been only twenty, anxious to live her dreams and get away from the mother who disapproved of everything she did.

The interior of the car fell silent, except for the wind squealing through the disintegrating window seals and the low rumble of the gas-guzzling engine. Kate knew she and her sister were delaying the obvious discussion. There was no easy way to go about it. The subject of their mother was like walking on cracked ice. No matter how lightly you tiptoed, you were bound to plunge into turbulent waters. Their mother had given birth to three children who had all moved away to different parts of the country. Each one had a completely different view of her parental skills.

Her death would bring them all together.

"After all the times we offered to buy her a new car I can't believe Mom still drove this old boat," Kate said.

"I can't believe it made it to the airport and back." Kelly tucked a stray blond lock behind her ear and let out a sigh. "Mom was funny about stuff, you know. She was the biggest 'if it ain't broke don't fix it' person I ever knew."

Was.

Knew.

As in past tense.

Kate glanced out the passenger window.

Her mother was gone.

No more worrying about what to send for Mother's

Day or Christmas or her birthday. No more chatter about the temperamental oven in their family bakery, or the dysfunctional quartet that made up the Founder's Day parade committee, or the latest gnome she'd discovered to stick in her vegetable garden.

No more . . . anything.

Almost a year had passed since she'd been with her mother. But even that hadn't been the longest she'd gone without seeing her. Kate had spent tons of time with Dean and Kelly. She'd snuck in a fishing trip or two with her dad. But an entire five years had gone by before Kate had finally agreed to meet up with her mother in Chicago to celebrate Kelly's promotion with the prosecutor's office. The reunion had been awkward. And as much as Kate had wanted to hear "I'm sorry" come from her mother's lips, she'd gone back to Los Angeles disappointed.

Over the years Kate had meant to come home. She'd meant to apologize. She'd meant to do a whole lot of stuff that just didn't matter anymore. Good intentions weren't going to change a thing. A knife of pain stabbed between her eyes. The time for could have, should have, would have, was history. Making amends was a two-way street and her mother hadn't made an effort either.

She shifted to a more comfortable position and her gaze landed on the cluttered chaos in the backseat—an array of pastry cookbooks, a box of quilting fabric, and a knitting tote where super-sized needles poked from the top of a ball of red yarn. Vanilla—her mother's occupational perfume—lingered throughout the car.

Kate inhaled. The scent settled into her soul and

jarred loose a long-lost memory. "Do you remember the time we all got chicken pox?" she asked.

"Oh, my God, yes." Kelly smiled. "We were playing tag. Mom broke up the game and stuck us all in one bedroom."

"I'd broken out with blisters first," Kate remembered, scratching her arm at the reminder. "Mom said if one of us got the pox, we'd all get the pox. And we might as well get it done and over with all at once."

"So *you* were the culprit," Kelly said.

"I don't even know where I got them." Kate shook her head. "All I know is I was miserable. The fever and itching were bad enough. But then you and Dean tortured me to see how far you could push before I cried."

"If I remember, it didn't take long."

"And if I remember," Kate said, "it didn't take long before you were both whining like babies."

"Karma," Kelly admitted. "And just when we were at our worst, Mom came in and placed a warm sugar cookie in each of our hands."

Kate nodded, remembering how the scent of vanilla lingered long after her mother had left the room. "Yeah."

The car rambled past Balloons and Blooms, the florist shop Darla Davenport had set up in her century-old barn.

"Dad ordered white roses for her casket." Kelly's voice wobbled. "He was concerned they wouldn't be trucked in on time and, of course, the price. I told him not to worry—that we kids would take care of the cost. I told him to order any damn thing he wanted."

Kate leaned forward and peered through her sister's sunglasses. "Are you okay?"

"Are you?" Kelly asked.

Instead of answering, Kate twisted off the cap of her Starbuck's Frappuccino and slugged down the remains. The drink gave her time to compose herself, if that were even possible. She thought of her dad. Simple. Hardworking. He'd taught her how to tie the fly that had helped her land the derby-winning trout the year she turned eleven. He couldn't have been more different from her mother if he'd tried. And he hadn't deserved to be abandoned by his youngest child.

"How's Dad doing?" Kate asked, as the iced drink settled in her stomach next to the wad of guilt.

"He's devastated." Kelly flipped on the fan. Her abrupt action seemed less about recirculating the air and more about releasing a little distress. "How would you be if the love of your life died in your arms while you were tying on her apron?"

"I can't answer that," Kate said, trying not to think about the panic that must have torn through him.

"Yeah." Kelly sighed. "Me either."

Kate tried to swallow but her throat muscles wouldn't work. She turned in her seat and looked at her sister. "What's he going to do now, Kel? Who will take care of him? He's never been alone. Ever," she said, her voice an octave higher than normal. "Who's going to help him at the Shack? Cook for him? Who's he going to talk to at night?"

"I don't know. But we definitely have to do something." Kelly nodded as though a lightbulb in her head suddenly hit a thousand watts. "Maybe Dean will have some ideas."

"Dean?" Kate leaned back in her seat. "Our brother? The king of non-relationship relationships?"

"Not that either of us has any room to talk."

"Seriously." Kate looked out the window, twisting the rings on her fingers. The urge to cry for her father welled in her throat. Her parents had been a great example of true love. They cared for each other, had each other's backs, thought of each other first. Even with her problematic relationship with her mother, Kate couldn't deny that the woman had been an extraordinary wife to the man who worshipped her. The chances of finding a love like the one her parents had shared were one in a million. Kate figured that left her odds stretching out to about one in a hundred gazillion.

"What's wrong with us, Kel?" she asked. "We were raised by parents the entire town puts on a pedestal, yet we all left them behind for something *bigger and better.* Not a single one of us has gotten married or even come close. As far as I know, Dean has no permanent designs on his current bimbo of the moment. You spend all your nights with a stack of law books. I spend too much time flying coast-to-coast to even meet up with someone for a dinner that doesn't scream fast food."

"Oh, poor you. New York to L.A. First Class. Champagne. And all those gorgeous movie stars and rock stars you're surrounded by. You're breaking my heart."

Kate snorted. "Yeah, I live such a glamorous life."

A perfectly arched brow lifted on Kelly's perfect face. "You don't?"

While Kate enjoyed what she did for a living, every day her career hung by a sequin while the next up-and-coming celebrity stylist waited impatiently in the wings for her to fall from Hollywood's fickle graces. She'd chosen a career that tossed her in the spotlight, but she had no one to share it with. And often that spotlight felt icy cold. "Yeah, sure. I just get too busy sometimes, you know?"

"Unfortunately, I do." Kelly gripped the wheel tighter. "You know . . . you could have stuck around and married Matt Ryan."

"Geez." Kate's heart did a tilt-a-whirl spin. "I haven't heard that name in forever."

"When you left, you broke his heart."

"How do you know?"

"Mom said."

"Hey, I gave him my virginity. I call that a fair trade."

"Seriously?" Kelly's brows lifted in surprise. "I had no idea."

"It wasn't something I felt like advertising at the time."

"He was pretty cute from what I remember."

"Don't go there, Kel. There's an ocean under that bridge. So mind your own business."

Matt Ryan. Wow. Talk about yanking up old memories. Not unpleasant ones either. From what Kate remembered, Matt had been very good at a lot of things. Mostly ones that involved hands and lips. But Matt had been that boy from the proverbial wrong side of the tracks and she'd had bigger plans for her life.

Her mother had only mentioned him once or twice after Kate had skipped town. Supposedly he'd eagerly moved on to all the other girls wrangling for his attention. Good for him. He'd probably gotten some poor girl pregnant and moved next door to his mother. No doubt he'd been saddled with screaming kids and a complaining wife. Kate imagined he'd still be working for his Uncle Bob fixing broken axles and leaky transmissions. Probably even had a beer gut by now. Maybe even balding. Poor guy.

Kelly guided their mother's boat around the last curve in the road that would lead them home. Quaking aspens glittered gold in the sunlight and tall pines dotted the landscape. Craftsman style log homes circled the area like ornaments on a Christmas wreath.

"Mom was proud of you, you know," Kelly blurted.

"What?" Kate's heart constricted. She didn't need for her sister to lie about their mother's mind-set. Kate knew the truth. She'd accepted it long ago. "No way. Mom did everything she could to pull the idea of being a celebrity stylist right out of my stubborn head."

"You're such a dork." Kelly shifted in her seat and gripped the steering wheel with both hands. "Of course she was proud. She was forever showing off the magazine articles you were in. She even kept a scrapbook."

"She did not."

"She totally did."

"Go figure. The night before I boarded that bus for

L.A., she swore I'd never make a living hemming skirts and teasing hair."

"No, what she said was, making a living hemming skirts and teasing hair wasn't for you," Kelly said.

"That's not the way I remember it."

"Of course not. You were so deeply immersed in parental rebellion she could have said the sky was blue and you'd have argued that it was aqua."

"We did argue a lot."

Kelly shook her head. "Yeah, kind of like you were both cut from the same scrap of denim. I think that's what ticked you off the most and you just didn't want to admit it."

No way. "That I was like Mom?"

"You could have been identical twins. Same red hair. Same hot temper."

"I never thought I was anything like her. I still don't."

"How's that river of denial working for you?"

"How's that rewriting history working for *you*?"

Kelly tightened her fingers on the steering wheel. "Someday you'll get it, little sister. And when you do, you're going to be shocked that you didn't see it earlier."

The remnants of the old argument curdled in Kate's stomach. "She didn't believe in me, Kel."

"Then she was wrong."

For some reason the acknowledgment from her big sister didn't make it any better.

"She was also wrong about you and your financial worth," Kelly added. "You make three times as much as I do."

"But not as much as Dean."

"God doesn't make as much as Dean," Kelly said.

Their big brother had always been destined for greatness. If you didn't believe it, all you had to do was ask him. Being an NFL star quarterback did have its perks. Modesty wasn't one of them.

"Almost there," Kelly announced.

The green highway sign revealed only two more miles to go. Kate gripped the door handle to steady the nervous tension tap-dancing on her sanity.

Ahead, she noticed the swirling lights atop a sheriff's SUV parked on the shoulder of the highway. The vehicle stopped in front of the cop had to be the biggest monster truck Kate had ever seen. In L.A., which oozed with hybrids and luxury cruisers, one could only view a farmboy-vehicle-hopped-up-on-steroids in box office bombs like the *Dukes of Hazzard*.

The swirling lights dredged up a not-so-fond memory of Sheriff Washburn, who most likely sat behind the wheel of that Chevy Tahoe writing up the fattest citation he could invent. A decade ago, the man and his Santa belly had come hunting for her. When she hadn't shown up at home at o'dark thirty like her mother had expected, the SOS call had gone out. Up on Lookout Point the sheriff had almost discovered her and Matt sans clothes, bathed in moonlight and lust.

As it was, Matt had been quick to act and she'd managed to sneak back through her bedroom window before she ruined her shaky reputation for all time. Turned out it wouldn't have mattered. A few days later she boarded a bus leaving that boy and the town gossips behind to commiserate with her mother about what an ungrateful child she'd been.

As they approached the patrol vehicle, a deputy stepped out and, hand on gun, strolled toward the monster truck.

Mirrored shades. Midnight hair. Wide shoulders. Trim waist. Long, long legs. And . . . Oh. My. God. Not even the regulation pair of khaki uniform pants could hide his very fine behind. Nope. Definitely *not* Sheriff Washburn.

A double take was definitely in order.

"Wow," Kate said.

"They didn't make 'em like that when we lived here," Kelly noted.

"Seriously." Kate shifted back around in her seat. And frowned. What the hell was wrong with her? Her mother had been dead for two days and *she* was checking out guys?

"Well, ready or not, here we are."

At her sister's announcement Kate looked up at the overhead sign crossing the two-lane road.

Welcome to Deer Lick, Montana. Population 6,000.

For Kate it might as well have read *Welcome to Hell.*

LATE THE FOLLOWING afternoon, Kate stood amid the mourners gathered at the gravesite for Leticia Jane Silverthorne's burial. Most were dressed in a variety of appropriate blacks and dark blues. The exception being Ms. Virginia Peat, who'd decided the bright hues of the local

Red Hat Society were more appropriate for a deceased woman with a green thumb and a knack for planting mischief wherever she went.

No doubt her mother had a talent for inserting just the right amount of monkey business into things to keep the town blabbing for days, even weeks, if the gossips were hungry enough. Better for business, she'd say. The buzz would catch on and the biddies of Deer Lick would flock to the Sugar Shack for tea and a sweet treat just to grab another tasty morsel of the brewing scandal.

Today, the Sugar Shack was closed. Her mother's cakes and pies remained unbaked. And the lively gossip had turned to sorrowful memories.

Beneath a withering maple, Kate escaped outside the circle of friends and neighbors who continued to hug and offer condolences to her father and siblings. Their almost overwhelming compassion notched up her guilt meter and served as a reminder of the small-town life she'd left behind. Which was not to say those in Hollywood were cold and unfeeling, she'd just never had any of them bring her hot chicken soup.

Plans had been made for a potluck gathering at the local Grange—a building that sported Jack Wagoner's award-winning moose antlers and held all the community events—including wedding receptions and the October Beer and Brat Fest. The cinder block structure had never been much to look at but obviously it remained the epicenter of the important events in beautiful downtown Deer Lick.

A variety of funeral casseroles and home-baked treats would be lined up on the same long tables used for arm wrestling competitions and the floral arranging contest held during the county fair. As far as Kate could see, not much had changed since she'd left. And she could pretty much guarantee that before the end of the night, some elder of the community would break out the bottle of huckleberry wine and make a toast to the finest pastry chef this side of the Rockies.

Then the stories would start to fly and her mother's name would be mentioned over and over along with the down and dirty details of some of her more outrageous escapades. Tears and laughter would mingle. Hankies would come out of back pockets to dab weeping eyes.

The truth hit Kate in the chest, tore at her lungs. The good people of Deer Lick had stood by her mother all these years while Kate had stood off in the distance.

She brushed a speck of graveside dust from the pencil skirt she'd picked up in Calvin Klein's warehouse last month. A breeze had cooled the late afternoon air and the thin material she wore could not compete. She pushed her sunglasses into place, did her best not to shiver, and tried to blend in with the surroundings. But the cost alone of her Louboutin peep toes separated her from the simple folk who dwelled in this town.

Maybe she should have toned it down some. She could imagine her mother shaking her head and asking who Kate thought she'd impress.

"Well, well, lookie who showed up after all."

Kate glanced over her shoulder and into the faded hazel eyes of Edna Price, an ancient woman who'd always reeked of moth balls and Listerine. The woman who'd been on the Founder's Day Parade committee alongside her mother for as long as Kate could remember.

"Didn't think you'd have the gumption," Edna said.

Gumption? Who used that word anymore?

Edna poked at Kate's ankles with a moose-head walking stick. "Didn't think you'd have the nerve," Edna enunciated as though Kate were either deaf or mentally challenged.

"Why would I need *nerve* to show up at my own mother's funeral?" *Oh, dumb question, Kate. Sure as spit the old biddy would tell her ten ways to Sunday why.*

The old woman leaned closer. Yep, still smelled like moth balls and Listerine.

"You left your dear sweet mama high and dry, what, twenty years ago?"

Ten.

"It's your fault she's where she is."

"*My* fault?" The accusation snagged a corner of Kate's heart and pulled hard. "What do you mean?"

"Like you don't know."

She had no clue. But that didn't stop her mother's oldest friend from piling up the charges.

"Broke her heart is what you did. You couldn't get up the nerve to come back when she was breathin'. Oh, no. You had to wait until—"

Kate's patience snapped. "Mrs. Price . . . you can

blame or chastise me all you want. But not today. Today, I am allowed to grieve like anyone else who's lost a parent. Got it?"

"Oh, I got it." Her pruney lips curled into a snarl. "But I also got opinions and I aim to speak them."

"Not today you won't." Kate lifted her sunglasses to the top of her head and gave Mrs. Price her best glare. "Today you will respect my father, my brother, and my sister. Or I will haul you out of this cemetery by your fake pearl necklace. Do I make myself clear?"

The old woman snorted then swiveled on her orthopedic shoes and hobbled away. Kate didn't mind taking a little heat. She was, at least, guilty of running and never looking back. But today belonged to her family and she'd be goddamned if she'd let anybody drag her past into the present and make things worse.

Great. And now she'd cursed on sacred ground.

Maybe just thinking the word didn't count. She already had enough strikes against her.

It's your fault. . .

Exactly what had Edna meant? How could her mother's death be any fault of hers when she'd been hundreds of miles away?

Kate glanced across the carpet of grass toward the flower-strewn mound of dirt. Beneath the choking scent of carnations and roses, beneath the rich dark soil, lay her mother.

Too late for good-byes.

Too late for apologies.

Things just couldn't get worse.

Unable to bear the sight of her mother's grave, Kate turned her head. She startled at the sudden appearance of the man in the khaki-colored deputy uniform who stood before her. She looked up—way up—beyond the midnight hair and into the ice blue eyes of Matt Ryan.

The boy she'd left behind.

Return to the Sugar Shack . . .

ANY GIVEN CHRISTMAS

When an injury dashes NFL Quarterback Dean Silverthorne's Super Bowl dreams, he heads back to Deer Lick, Montana, with a chip on his wounded shoulder and more determined than ever to get back in the game. He loves his kooky family, but his trip home is nothing but a very brief Christmas visit.

His game plan didn't include an instant attraction to Emma Hart, a feisty kindergarten teacher, who seems to be the only person in Deer Lick not interested in the hometown hero. Or his dearly departed mom popping up with mistletoe in hand and meddling on the mind. Now Dean can't help but wonder if there's more to love than life between the goal posts.

Available now wherever e-books are sold.

SOMEBODY LIKE YOU

Letty Silverthorne has her work cut out for her when her middle child, Kelly, returns home to Deer Lick reeling from a major courtroom loss and needing to shake the "Sister Serious" moniker she's been carried since childhood. With the help of her dead mother and a former bad boy in uniform, anything is possible at the Sugar Shack.

Coming in June 2012 from Avon Impulse!

About the Authors

CATHY MAXWELL spends hours in front of her computer pondering the question, "Why do people fall in love?" It remains for her the greatest mystery of life and the secret to happiness. She lives in beautiful Virginia with children, horses, dogs, and cats. And if you imagine that you have met William Duroy before, it's because you have. He was first introduced to readers in *Treasured Vows*. Fans can contact Cathy at www.cathymaxwell.com or PO Box 1135, Powhatan, VA 23139.

A retreat leader and writing teacher, **LYNNE HINTON** is the author of numerous novels including *Pie Town*, *Wedding Cake*, *Christmas Cake*, *Friendship Cake*, *Hope Springs*, and *Forever Friends*. She also writes a mystery series under the name Jackie Lynn. She lives in New Mexico. She can be reached at www.lynnehinton.com.

CANDIS TERRY was born and raised near the sunny beaches of Southern California and now makes her home on an Idaho farm. She's experienced life in such diverse ways as working in a Hollywood recording studio to scooping up road apples left by her daughter's rodeo queening horse to working as a graphic designer. Only one thing has remained constant: Candis's passion for writing stories about relationships, the push and pull in the search for love, and the security one finds in their own happily-ever-after. Though her stories are set in small towns, Candis's wish is to give each of her characters a great big memorable love story rich with quirky characters, tons of fun, and a happy ending. For more, please visit www.candisterry.com.

OPERATION PAPERBACK

Avon Books is proud to salute America's armed forces!

This Memorial Day, in celebration of *For Love and Honor*, we will be donating books to Operation Paperback, a non-profit organization that collects books and sends them to American troops deployed overseas, and to SOS Aloha, the blog site for SOS America, an internet destination dedicated to promoting romance books to military families and military issues to romance readers.

For more information about these organizations, please visit:

http://www.operationpaperback.org/

http://www.sosamericainc.org/

http://sosaloha.blogspot.com/

www.facebook.com/avonromance